To Jeanne
Thanks for reading !

The
Sneaky Freaky

2022

by Carol Ann Ross

D1247498

IRONHEAD PRESS

Cover design by Carol Ann Ross and Deb McKnight.

This novel is a work of fiction. Names, characters,
and incidents are a product of the author's
imagination and are used fictitiously. Any
resemblance to actual events or persons, living or
dead, is purely coincidental.

ACKNOWLEDGEMENTS

Thanks to Evelyn Hobbs, Steve Midgett, Mary Ellen Rochelle, Randy Batts, Deborah Batts, and Diane Batts for searching your memories of Topsail and Sneads Ferry.

Thank you Deb McKnight, Elizabeth O'Brian, and Marlene Bottoms for your time and opinions. Thanks also to Taylor Williams, the hippie gal on the cover, for posing and offering so much personality.

Special thanks to the Vietnam Vets Guss Imperio, Craig Fedor, Terry Blackburn, Ray Fettinger, and Joe Mayfield, for all the information and honesty. Thank you for serving our country and for the sacrifices you made. We are indebted to you beyond measure.

DEDICATION

To the brave men and women of the Vietnam War

BOOKS BY CAROL ANN ROSS

Murder by the Sea Series
Waterlogged
Bridge Tender
The Tower
The Mermaid Did It
Shark's Breath
All These Little Things
Tickler Chain

Topsail Island Trilogy
The Days of Hairawn Muhly
The Trill of the Red Wing Blackbird
The Bridge to Paradise

The Blue House Series
Topsail Island Tango
The Sneaky Freaky

Standalone Novels
Plum Duff
Pelagic

Everyone is broken, that's how the light gets in.

- Ernest Hemingway

CHAPTER 1

Autumn 1966

It was a dark and stormy night, the wind howled through ….

Naomi read the first few words of the novel she'd selected from the library and rolled her eyes. She heard the rumble of thunder outside her window and growled, "It *is* going to be a dark and stormy night."

Her eyes returning to the page, she searched for the last sentence she'd read.

Lucy heard the soft footsteps on the stairs, the creak from the one step, and she pulled the covers up to her neck. It was the third step from the top that always creaked. She bit her bottom lip and thought of the gun in the drawer in the cabinet across the room.

"Oh, gee whiz," Naomi snorted as she closed the cover and thought of how cliche the story sounded. Surely, the worn first words were an indication that the novel was going to stink. Still, she read on, covering a few more paragraphs before curling her lip and setting the book on the nightstand.

Crossing her arms across her abdomen, Naomi exhaled a disgusted sigh and watched the curtains billow against the gusts of wind coming in through the window. She thought of closing it for a moment, then thought against it, since often times, storms or signs of storms came and went without a drop of rain. She heard another rumble in the distance, glanced at the book, the billowing curtains, and let her mind wander to Roy, her husband. His picture sat on the bureau across from the bed and as her eyes found his face, she smiled at the thought of the day he'd had the picture taken and the way his lips had sneered. *My hair's all gone,* he'd said as he had brushed his hand across his buzz cut hair.

Roy's hair was beautiful, at least it had been before the Marines. He'd let the bangs grow long and just a bit over his ears, so the brassy, sun-streaked locks framed his wide face. Despite the nagging and ridicule from his family and friends, Roy had taken pride in his shaggy look.

Naomi felt the sinking feeling she'd been battling since he'd been shipped out, and shook her head and turned it to stare at the dark screen of the television.

"Nothing good on," she hissed as she picked up the remote control. She giggled then, as she thought of how nice it was not having to get out of bed to change the channel; she kissed the air. "Thank you, Sweetie, for the remote."

Then her eyes widened at the scene of red blood spurting from a flesh-colored neck. Blue eyes rolled back into the head of a blonde *femme fetale*, and a scream burst through the air from the actress's red-lipsticked mouth. No, Naomi wasn't quite used to color television yet.

She flipped to the next channel, where some old black and white monster movie was playing. She watched the creature lumber its seaweed-draped body from the black lagoon.

"Ugh," she sounded, and flipped to the only other channel available, where the news was on. It was just as scary, perhaps even more so, as the horror movies she'd flipped past.

"Vietnam," Dan Rather, the handsome CBS reporter, held a microphone to his mouth and spoke, *"… is a …."* Naomi pointed the remote at the television, clicking the off button. She didn't want to hear about Vietnam. She wanted to sleep.

"War and monsters," she groaned as she stared at the dark screen of her television. Her mind wandered into nothingness. She thought of how, earlier, she'd watched *It's the Great Pumpkin, Charlie Brown.* It had made her laugh, had taken her thoughts away from the fact that she was alone, and that not only was her husband in Vietnam, but so was her brother.

Sighing, she turned her attention to the curtains, now flailing wildly as gusts of wind blew through the open window. The smell of salt air burst through as well, bringing with it a bit of late October chill. She pulled the quilt folded at the bottom of the bed toward her and turned the television back on, clicking back to the first channel she'd tried.

The horror movie was gone and in its place were the opening credits to *Arsenic and Old Lace.* It was just beginning.

"Ah," Naomi smiled as she watched the credits scroll the names Cary Grant, Raymond Massey and Peter Lorre. Yes, it was another Halloween movie, but what else could she expect? It would be Halloween in two weeks. Besides, the movie would be funny and more than anything other than sleep, Naomi needed to laugh.

Fluffing her pillow, Naomi pulled the quilt forward and folded it to her waist and watched Cary Grant's character bumble his way through the door and meet up with his girlfriend, Elaine. She listened to the chatty conversation between the two actors. Then came the first commercial.

The color commercial made her mouth salivate as an apron-clad homemaker rolled out the piecrust dough she had made with Crisco, *just as flaky as grandma's homemade pies,* the woman said.

"Pie," Naomi announced to the room. Quickly she threw back the covers of her bed, slipped her feet into a pair of fluffy pink slippers and reached for the pink chenille robe draped across the vanity chair. The blueberry pie Mim had brought over earlier in the day would be great with a glass of milk.

Naomi eyed the alarm clock as she rose. 1:15. She needed to be ready for Mim to pick her up at seven-thirty. "What a gem," she tittered aloud.

Not everybody would drive all the way from Surf City to Sneads Ferry to pick me up, she thought. *She's always been a sweet little girl.*

The rumbling outside was unmistakable, louder now, as Naomi descended the stairs. She hurried her steps, one, hoping to not miss much of the movie, and two, because it really was going to be *a dark and stormy night*. The bedroom windows would have to be closed after all. She shivered as she spotted the silent fingers of lightning through the living room window and felt her aloneness.

The home seemed so much bigger than it once had, when she and Roy had done the walk-through before deciding to buy. Then it had been perfect: three bedrooms, one for she and Roy, one for a boy child and one for a girl. That was the plan, a perfect family, settled in a waterfront home, white picket fence around the front and back yard. Maybe a dog, a Labrador or poodle.

Her mind's eye saw it all, and of course the sun was shining. Roy was in his swimsuit, calling from the dock where their Grady White with the cuddy cabin sat bobbing on the water. *Are the kids ready?* she heard him say.

They would be motoring down the Intracoastal Waterway, and they'd stop at the north end of Topsail Island for a picnic.

She sighed at the thought and felt the old boards of the house creak as she reached the bottom step. The rattle and scratch of the leafless crepe myrtle against a window startled her as she moved from the dining room into the kitchen, and she glimpsed the silhouette of the branches jerking about in the heavy breeze.

The swinging door to the kitchen screeched as it swung back and forth, and Naomi mouthed the word *oil*, reminding herself that she would need to buy a can. Inhaling the faint citrus aroma of the bowl of lemons on the counter, Naomi giggled.

"It's just rain and thunder, no need …." The neighbor's cat caterwauled outside the kitchen door. "Damn cat," she muttered, "why don't they get that thing fixed, or feed it or something? It spends more time over here than over there."

She thought for a moment, wondering if the cat actually did belong to her neighbor, the one that was two empty lots down from her. "Or somebody's," she groaned, "it's too tame to be feral."

Lifting the lace curtains, she peered from the window and spied the black feline. A few raindrops had fallen on its fur. She tapped on the glass. "Scat, cat." One florescent orb shone almost purple as it looked back at her, and the wide, gaping mouth full of pointed tines meowed back. "Shoo, you're going to get wet." Naomi pursed her lips and turned away.

Turning her attention to the refrigerator, she pulled the uneaten pie from a shelf and cut a large portion. "Ooh, ice-cream too," she cooed, and opened the freezer door to reach for the tub of Maola's Creamy Vanilla in the corner. She smiled again, then jumped as the sound of thunder cut through the air.

"Oh fiddlesticks, it's just a storm, silly," Naomi cried as she rushed to return the food to the refrigerator. The flat notes of the cat pierced the air again, and she grabbed a left-over piece of chicken from the refrigerator. "Damn cat." She peered out the window once more. *Pitickity*, that's the name her landlord had told her, was still there, rubbing his body against a post, meowing, his one glazed eye nearly as spooky as the other, florescent one.

Naomi heard another crack of thunder and watched fingers of light spread through the sky as she opened the door and tossed the leg outside.

"Here, Pitickity." Cold, thick drops of rain splashed against her skin and she slammed the door quickly. Watching from the window, she saw the cat, chicken leg in tow, bound across the yard. Her eyes scanning the dark, wet, sky, Naomi tightened the belt of her robe.

"Not a star, not a single star," she mumbled, then took the stairs to her bedroom, veering off to the right to check the upstairs bathroom and the metal pot she kept there for nights just like this. No water had dripped from the ceiling into it, yet. She centered the pot again, best she could, beneath the discolored wooden ceiling slats and closed the door behind her.

The lights flickered for a moment as thunder rumbled once again, and Naomi thought of the oil lamp in the cupboard in the kitchen, the candle in the hall and the flashlight in her room. She nodded an affirmation of readiness if the need be, and heard the unmistakable voice of Cary Grant screech in fear. The sound echoed down the hall and Naomi rushed to close the window in her room, then to scurry beneath the covering, tittering the whole while as she anticipated at least a couple of hours of laughter and respite from the buzz of thoughts in her head.

CHAPTER 2

It's fifty-five degrees this morning but by one o'clock temperatures should rise into the mid-seventies ….

Naomi wakened to the words from the WECT weatherman, Jim Burns. She yawned and, noticing the empty plate resting beside her, mumbled and grinned. "Thank you Mim, you're a good cook."

Must have fallen asleep while …. Naomi sighed as she pulled herself up, fluffed her pillows and leaned back against the headboard. She glanced at the clock, which read 6:05. *Guess I got a few hours of sleep.* Her brow furrowed as she tried to recall the last scene from the movie she'd been watching. Naomi laughed aloud at the thought of the Brewster sisters and their homemade elderberry wine.

"It must have been almost over," she said aloud. "So maybe four hours of sleep? Oh well, that's enough." Then she groaned as she noticed the pie crust crumbs scattered where she had been sleeping. What was that her mother-in-law had said during her last visit? *Cleanliness is next to godliness.*

"What does that old biddy know about God? She's mean as a snake." Eyeing the crumbs again as she rose, Naomi grumbled, "I can't do anything right, according to you, Lenore. Well, you ain't here are you, you old bat?"

Naomi's eyes flew to the framed picture turned backwards on the wall and thought of Lenore Simpson, her husband's mother, and the wedding picture.

"Neh, neh, neh, family picture my eye. You sure did make sure none of my family was in the photo, didn't you... *humph*." Naomi scrunched her nose and slid her toes into the thick fibers of gold shag carpeting and rose from the bed.

Slipping on her robe, she padded barefoot to the bathroom. Studying her unkempt image in the mirror, she reached to turn the knobs of the shower. She stretched the elastic shower cap over her thick hair and thought, *I've got about an hour before Mim comes--plenty of time.*

She languished in the shower, knowing that it would only take her a few minutes to dress. Leaning against the wall of the shower, she closed her eyes to the image of Roy, her husband of five years. Oh, he was handsome, especially in his cracker jacks. The way his tunic rested on his shoulders, the cut of the bell bottom trousers holding tightly against his slim waist. Naomi giggled again.

She never had been a fool for the flattery of young men. But his flattery had been different, it had been love at first sight. Roy, the most handsome star player on the Dixon team and Naomi, the prettiest cheerleader on the Topsail team, it was a romance that could have been made in Hollywood.

No one was surprised when they married a month after graduation, but unlike some of the other kids who had married early, they had no children. There had been no draft notice either, at first. When it came two years later, Roy had joined the Navy. After testing high in triangulating distances, he had been sent to Pensacola, Florida and then to Tennessee where he'd trained for several weeks before being sent to Vietnam, where he flew as a navigation bombardier.

I'm safer up there than anywhere, Roy had assured his wife. *I'm in the Navy, the safest branch and safest profession.*

Naomi giggled as she worked the wash cloth against her skin, seeing Roy's smile in her mind's eye. Then, as quickly as his smile had come, it left and that last day's ache filled her. The newscast she'd watched several weeks ago about casualties of innocent women and children played in her head. She shook her head against it as she thought of Roy caught in the gunfire reported so often on the nightly news.

"No," she called out.

The decision had been made, and Naomi would stick to it. She would not think about the bad things, she would listen to no news about Vietnam, she would walk away from anyone deriding the war and the men fighting there. Pressing her hands against her ears, Naomi slid slowly down the walls of the shower and, holding her knees to her chest, sobbed.

* * * *

"Thanks for driving all the way out here to pick me up, Mim."

"We are the only two out of the class who live north of Hampstead," Mim offered as she stood beside the Mustang. "Besides, I like driving down here. It's pretty. You've got a great view of the river." She walked to the side of the house and, peering south to the bend in the landscape, asked, "That's the Intracoastal, right?"

Naomi nodded. "Yes, it turns into the ICW right past that bend and takes you to the inlet and out into the ocean." Her eyes twinkled. "Roy and I have made the ICW our second home, we spend so much time on it."

"And that--" Mim pointed across the water to the gathering of brick buildings, "--that's Court

House Bay, Camp Lejeune? Wonder how many pass through there before going to Vietnam?"

"No idea," Naomi exhaled an annoyed breath and changed the subject. "How about that storm last night?"

"What storm? Oh, I heard a little rumbling, but it never did rain on the island. It rained here?"

"Lucky you, lightning was popping and the wind, it was crazy. It rained cats and dogs, not a star in the sky. It scared the bee gee bees out of me and to boot, that creepy old cat from next door came caterwauling at the door. I swear, that is the ugliest cat I've ever seen."

"Ah, poor cat, it's just miserable."

"Pitickity, poor Pitickity," Naomi giggled. "What a strange name, and ugly as mud." Scrunching her nose, she continued, "It must be terrible having to be that ugly and unwanted." She laughed. "That girl from Southport ought to know about that."

Mim knew the girl Naomi meant; she kind of reminded her of Kellie, the earlier Kellie with pimples and a paunch. "She is sort of homely, reminds me of my friend Kellie, you remember her, don't you? She's in Vietnam now." Mim started, "Isn't Roy...?"

Naomi cleared her throat, opened the car door and slid inside. Picking up the big blue text book, she read the title, *Proper Etiquette*. "Yes, that's something I'm going to need here in Sneads Ferry."

A thin smile crossed her lips and she added, "You know there's going to be a test this morning. Mrs. Baker always gives etiquette quizzes on Mondays." Her attention turned pointedly away from Mim, then, as she opened the book.

Mim looked quizzically to Naomi; she could feel the coolness. And though their relationship had become more friendly, Mim was sure they would never be besties like she and Kellie. Sighing, she stored the questions about Naomi and Roy's life away, and, pressing her foot down on the accelerator, sped Kellie's baby blue Mustang up to fifty-five miles per hour after she turned on to Highway 17.

They drove in silence, Mim somewhat miffed at the cold shoulder. Fumbling with the radio dial, she thought, *Naomi has fallen from grace. Miss hoity toity, she was the girl with everything and has now had her comeuppance. She peaked in high school.*

Mim slid an eye to study Naomi for a moment. Her hair was still beautiful, still in the bouffant style, but there was less eye shadow and practically no mascara. The pert and cheerful girl she'd known in high school had become aloof and diffident. At Miller Motte, the secretarial college, she was quiet and demur, and so unlike the somewhat sassy girl she'd been at Topsail High school, the one who flirted in the hallways and primped in front of the girls.

The pretty ones always end up fat and ugly, Mim thought. She had heard that from Sharon, the waitress at the Breeze-way where she and her mother had gone for lunch a few days before.

Only jealous people talk like that, her momma had said later.

You're right, Momma, Mim thought as she drove. *I barely know her and her husband. I guess I have no right to judge.*

Mim remembered passing the older girl in the hall, never speaking, yet acknowledging her arrogant, though care-free attitude and her obvious popularity. The boys had always turned their heads when Naomi had passed and the girls, well, if they weren't her friend, they were the ones throwing the dirty looks and gossiping. She had been Topsail's "it" girl.

Naomi had been the first to wear bouffant style hairdos. The first to wear eye shadow, eyeliner and loads of mascara, and the first to wear a miniskirt. Mim recalled when Naomi had been called to the office. News of a reprimand for the short miniskirt had flown down the grapevine of gossipers in the school before homeroom had ended. Supposedly, Adele Cartwright, Naomi's mother, had been waiting with an appropriate length skirt for her to wear. Still, regardless of the dress code, things slacked a bit, and by the end of the school year, all the girls were wearing short skirts.

Naomi had been class president and, in the yearbook, voted prettiest. She had been a cheerleader, in the Beta Club and Glee Club. In school plays, she had always played the lead and at talent contests she had played either the piano or flute. Always the best dressed and most hip dresser for small-town Topsail School, Naomi had worn the latest fashions from Raleigh, where she and her mother had traveled every three months.

Had she been jealous of Naomi? Mim thought not. *Was she jealous of her now?* If she was, it was not about popularity or looks; Mim felt fairly confident there. But she did feel a bit envious of the way Naomi was in control. Whatever was going on in her life, Naomi did not feel the need for sharing. She did not wear her heart on her sleeve and kept her love life, her frustrations, to herself. Mim did envy Naomi's self-control. If the older girl had failed at anything, she had never let it show.

And here was Mim, two years younger than Naomi, and had already been married and divorced, and now with a crush on some guy who barely spoke to her. She'd been stupid enough to let some fifteen-year-old kid kiss her and had been in a car wreck where someone had died. That sounded like a lot of mistakes to Mim, and she felt embarrassed about them.

Compared to Naomi, her ducks were wandering all around the yard. Naomi's ducks were in in a proper row, kept there by some sense of purpose, or whatever it was. Naomi was doing things with her life, going to secretarial school and making the house she and Roy were buying into a home. She was obviously preparing for her future. The flower garden in the front yard was perfect. The symmetry of the different flowers made it apparent that someone had spent hours planting and weeding and making everything just so. Now, in the fall, the pansies and asters had been assorted and arranged to form a rainbow's arc of color. The monkey grass edging near the base of the picket fence had been trimmed to just a few inches above the lawn that Naomi kept mowed. *Just where does she find time to work at the Riverview Restaurant too?* thought Mim.

Against the quietness of the drive, Mim spoke. "Your yard is beautiful, you must have a green thumb."

Naomi shrugged, adding a thank you.

"And the collards you let me try for lunch the other day were great."

Again, Naomi shrugged and mouthed a thank you.

"For the life of me, I just cannot cook collards. They always turn out leathery and taste like salted, greasy nothing. When Momma cooks them, they're great. When I cook them they taste like an old shoe." Mim chuckled lightly. "So, what's the secret Naomi? Where do you get yours?"

Lifting her head from the book, Naomi slid her eyes to Mim. "If you must know, I think some kid steals them for the Simpsons. Roy's father brought them already cooked up for me. He laughed about it and said that collards were the only meal he knew how to cook--said he stole the collards out of some farmer's patch." Naomi snickered. "I thought he was joking when he said he stole them, but Roy told me it was true. I guess that's all they have to do around here, steal collards." Once again, she turned her attention to the book.

Why so secretive? Mim scowled as she thought. *She doesn't want to talk about Roy, the cat, or collards, or anything.* Her eyes widened at the recollection of Naomi referring to Sneads Ferry as the sneaky freaky a few days ago and she let out an audible "*Ha*. Oh, I get it, collard stealing in the sneaky freaky. Is that it?"

Mim waited for a response, in vain. Tired of being ignored by someone she was going out of her way to help, Mim asked again, "So, why is Sneads Ferry called sneaky freaky?"

Naomi's hooded lids slid away from the tome she was reading, and to Mim. She shrugged. "Beats me. I haven't the slightest clue." Turning her head back to the big blue book, she flipped another page.

Mim mused as she drove through the town of Hampstead, wondering, as her peripheral vision caught Naomi with head still down, *How does she do that, read in the car? If I did that, I'd puke all over the place.* A few minutes passed and Mim realized that no pages had been flipped. *She's not reading at all.*

For a moment, she felt sorry for Naomi and wondered what she must be going through with her husband so far away, fighting in a war that was becoming more and more unpopular. There were reports that American troops were massacring villages of people and that bombs were being dropped on innocents. Wasn't Naomi's husband a bombardier? Wasn't her brother a Marine fighting in Vietnam? Mim wondered if all she was hearing on the news was true. But she'd heard from others that Americans were being blamed for things that guerilla troops from Korea were doing.

Mim heard so many stories on the news every night about the fighting and the count of wounded and dead. She had listened to the commentators expressing views she did not fully understand and she'd listened to opinions from Roger and other Marines from Camp Lejeune. Mim wondered what she should believe. Everything was changing, and changing fast. Certainly, she had changed since high school, but so had Naomi, who was now so much more aloof, as if she didn't want to be bothered. As if she wanted to keep the rest of the world away from her life. She was nothing like the carefree, popular girl from high school. Had the war changed her too?

Even the day Mim had dropped by with the blueberry pie, Naomi had seemed guarded. Continuing to work in the front yard flower garden, she had remained crouched at the pansies, weeding, offering a superficial smile, and straightening her husband's sailor hat. As if by memory, she had begun recounting plans she and Roy had for their home, the yard, and how things would be ready for him when he returned.

Had she been nervous then? Surprised? Did I interrupt something? Mim asked herself as she drove. *She took me on the tour*, Mim recalled. They'd entered the two-story house with Naomi explaining how old the house was, and how it needed repairs, so she couldn't show off the upstairs. She had talked about the master bedroom, and how it was already a pale blue. The other rooms had not been painted yet and the upstairs bathroom was a mess. Naomi had gone on to say that the fourth room would be either a study for Roy or sewing room for her and again, no colors had been decided for those either.

Naomi had walked her through the downstairs; the kitchen was beautiful with shiny, white linoleum flooring, striped yellow and white curtains, and a yellow Formica table sitting in the center of the room. A bowl of yellow lemons had been centered there.

Then it had been into the dining room, Naomi talking the whole while about what she and Roy had planned and what they wanted. She had asked Mim to take special notice of the small chandelier hanging above an oak table with eight chairs. *Do you think it's too small?* she had asked. A vase of fresh cut flowers had been centered on this table.

Naomi's decorating throughout the part of the house Mim had seen had been simple. There were still life prints on the walls in the kitchen, and in the living room, Naomi had pointed out the original painting of an ocean scene, from an artist from Raleigh, hanging over the fireplace. Matching, avocado-colored wing back chairs had sat on either side, contrasting well with the shag carpeting.

And this is the den, where the family--where we watch TV, Naomi had started. She'd moved close to the Curtis Mathes console, the focal point of the room. Naomi had opened the cabinet doors to reveal the television and the high-fidelity radio and record player. The carved cherry wood structure had to have been close to six feet long. A long, black leather couch had faced the console with hassocks at each end. The room had looked very hip and modern with the padded half-moon bar in the corner, with glass decanters of what Mim assumed to be alcohol. There had been a star-shaped clock on the wall right behind the bar.

With each room, Naomi's composure had eased more and she had become more friendly, and had even touched Mim's shoulder. She had become more relaxed, more talkative with Mim as they'd moved through the rooms. Finally, Naomi had smiled and explained how she and Roy planned on decorating certain rooms and even changing the outside. She had explained that Mr. Bolton, their landlord, the man who was allowing them to rent-to-own their home, would come around sometimes and help her in the yard and fix little odds and ends that needed mending. She had gone on and on about her and Roy's plans. The more she had talked about Roy, the more relaxed Naomi had become. She had been especially cheery when she'd spoken of how often they motored to the little islands in the Intracoastal Waterway and near the north inlet to Topsail, where they picked up pieces of driftwood to decorate the back yard.

Truthfully, the backyard had been Mim's favorite. A net had been hung against a back wall, with round glass buoy balls threaded through the netted material. Starfish and seahorses were positioned here and there as well. Large pieces of driftwood were situated around a brick grill, with old stumps set around it for seating.

It had all looked very cozy to Mim and she'd felt herself excited for the prospect that someday, when Naomi's husband came back home, she would be invited to one of the cookouts.

Naomi had gone on and on, repeating herself, talking about Roy's last visit a few months earlier. It had been the first time they'd seen each other in ten months. She'd talked about how good he had looked, how they'd gone clamming, how they'd gone to the north end of Topsail Island and gathered driftwood, but then abruptly, the story had ended, as had her enthusiasm.

What was it? Mim wondered as she looked back on that day. *Did I say something inappropriate? Had Naomi suddenly recalled something? Whatever it was, it stopped Naomi in her tracks and that was the end of that. She shooed me out the door and thanked me for the pie.*

Mim had asked no questions. But she did wonder about her friend. On the outside, it looked like Naomi had everything. She had the looks, the man, the house, it seemed that she wanted for nothing. *What makes her tick?* Mim thought as she glanced over to Naomi.

CHAPTER 3

Would she be looking at the sky? Roy asked himself. *Of course she will be.* Roy's eyes scanned the sky and, locating the celestial equator, found Orion, the hunter in Greek mythology. Noticing the brightest stars as they flickered, he wrote down the time; it was 20:30 hours. He'd taught her military time at her insistence.

His eyes searched again, this time for Cassiopeia. It was easy to find since it was shaped like a big W. It was a winter constellation, seen better during that time of year, and since Naomi could identify the Big Dipper easily in the sky, all she had to do was look above it and there it would be.

Roy's eyes caught the flare of heat lightning, or was it bombing? He rested against the ship, holding a pen and pad, and scrawled, *My dearest Naomi, have you been watching the stars? Have you seen how bright Cassiopeia is now? It will be even brighter as winter comes. I think about you all the time.*

He wrote more about how he missed his wife and how boring it was staring at water all day and how it was nice to see how the dolphins played along the sides of the ship as it moved along.

Had to go ashore the other day to do some scouting. I was dressed for it, but you know, being so tall, I stuck out like a sore thumb. Don't think I've hunched over so much in my life, ha ha ... don't worry, the trip was pretty innocuous. Yep, learned another big word. Innocuous means nothing bad happened, it was pretty safe.

Have you seen much of my mom? I know she can be kind of bossy sometimes, but she's not so bad, just ignore her little comments. When she writes me it's always about how she misses me and how she hates being alone. Since she and Dad separated, it seems she takes everything out on everybody else. Maybe you could visit her sometime, when you get the car fixed and can make the drive to Raleigh.

Well, I know you don't see my father much. He's busy fishing and this is the season for mackerel and blue fish. But I guess he's catching mostly black fish. It's a good market for them now. This time last year when I was home, we went out to Fifteen Mile Rock and caught so many fish we had to stuff the scuppers with boots cause the fish were overflowing the boxes and we had to dump them on deck.

31

Can't wait to get back on leave and go to Topsail Island, take the Grady White down the Intracoastal, maybe even go to Lea Island like we used to for a picnic.

Remember the time we went to Figure Eight Island and looked at all the big houses they're building over there? Hope you're keeping the boat ship-shape for me while I'm gone. Just a little elbow grease on the hull will keep her pretty. Make sure to always take the gas can in the garage when you leave the boat. You know how things are. Lots of sticky fingers down there. Ha ha!

I'll write again in a couple of days. Can't wait to hear from you. I know you're doing a great job at the house and making it our home.

Signing his name with love, he folded the pages, slipped them into the envelope and reached for another piece of paper to start a letter to his mother.

Dear Mom, it's been quiet over here. Not much action. I saw a nice doll in Saigon when I was there on leave a few weeks ago. It will make a nice addition to your collection. I'll try to pick it up for you next time I get over there.

Hope you and Dad are taking care of the Barracuda. Naomi has her hands full with the house, getting it fixed up, so I know you don't mind making sure it gets driven at least a couple times a month. I know Dad is keeping oil in it. Wish you would let her use it.

Naomi sent me pictures of the front yard, she is working hard to make it look good and the house look nice.

I want you to know I appreciate all that you do too.

I know you spend a lot of time in Raleigh, wish you and Dad wouldn't fight so much.

Well, have to go.

All my love, your son,

Roy

He'd been dealing with his mother's criticism about Naomi's house cleaning since they got married. But it didn't end there. Lenore Simpson complained about anything and everything. She hated Sneads Ferry, she hated fishing and anything to do with it, despite the fact that the fine home and bulging bank account were due to her husband's fishing business. She complained all the time, unless it was when she was making a trip to Raleigh, which was where she was planning on moving to as soon as the divorce was final. At least, that is what she'd told her son.

Roy shook his head as he thought of his mother. In the last couple of years, he'd come to realize that his father's words to her had been true: *Nobody's good enough for your precious son, and there's just no pleasing you.* He was ready for his parents' divorce and believed his father would be much happier without the nagging and complaining of his mother.

Roy's letters to her were short, though he did try to make them comforting. He wrote a few lines and signed them with love. He would drop a line to his father later.

Exhaling, he thought of how nice it would have been if his mother were fonder of Naomi, if she would have found at least a couple of things about his wife to praise. But she blamed Naomi for changing him, taking him away from her, and for his decision stay in Sneads Ferry and fish rather than attending college. His father, Al, had never pushed for it; he was proud Roy was following in his footsteps and had chosen fishing for his livelihood.

Fishermen made a good living in Sneads Ferry. Sure, it was a lot of hard work, but it paid off. And as long as people ate seafood, he'd always have a job. Alfred Simpson was proud of his son for choosing to be part of the family business, for serving his country and for putting money down on a house. It might have been fifty years old, with a creaky stairway and a roof that leaked, but it was his, or at least on the way to being his. Norwood Bolton was selling it for a song.

"You caught him on a good day," Al had told Roy. "Next week he might change his mind, you know he ain't got no nails for his hammer." Roy laughed as he thought of his father's euphemism. But it was true, as kind as Norwood was, he could also be a little unconventional. Whatever the case, Roy had felt lucky that he'd caught Norwood on a day when he had been willing to do a rent-to-own deal with only two hundred dollars down.

The two-story house would make a nice home once it was remodeled and full of kids. That's what both he and Naomi wanted, and if it had been up to him alone, they would already have a couple. But Naomi wanted to wait and had started the pill.

So here he was in Vietnam, sitting on an aircraft carrier, flying missions over Nam and even getting shot at sometimes. Life was not supposed to be this way, and for a moment he wondered if he had done the wrong thing by not going to college; with that would have come a deferment.

****

Dearest Roy, the other night we had a horrible thunderstorm. There wasn't a star in the sky, but I do look up every night and look for Cassiopeia and Ursa Major. I'm learning right along with you and I find it funny that we're learning the constellations while you are on a ship named Constellation. *Well, the lightning was popping everywhere during the storm and that doggone cat from next door (Mr. Bolton says its name is Pitickity) was meowing its*

*head off. I swear, I just don't understand why those
people next door don't feed that poor thing. And its
eye, you know the one, well, it's just spooky as all
get out. Maybe I'll get a pair of eyeglasses, frost one
over and go as that cat for Halloween at the church.
I know it's just for kids but Vickie Smalley is taking
her kids and asked me to tag along. I'll let you know
how it turns out.*

*Your mother dropped by the other day too. I
don't think she likes me one little bit. But I will try,
my love, I try very hard to be nice. She criticizes
everything I do; I can't seem to do anything right.
But maybe with time, and like you say, once we have
kids it will change. I hope you're right.*

*My friend Mim, she's the girl who was a couple
of grades behind me at Topsail, made me a
blueberry pie. Why? Don't ask me, she just said she
felt like baking a pie and knew I liked blueberries.
She also drove over from Surf City the morning after
the storm to take me to school. The pie was good
and comforting during the storm. I watched an old
movie with Cary Grant in it,* Arsenic and Old Lace. *It
wasn't in color. Seems weird watching in color, it
makes everything so life-like. I sure do like that color
television we bought at the PX when you were home
on leave and I love the remote control.*

*Sure do wish the movie would have been in
color, but that's okay, it was still funny.*

The Chevy broke down again (that's why Mim had to come over and get me) and I'm hoping Guy's Garage in Fulcher's Landing can fix it quick. Mr. Guy says it's the transmission and it might cost a bit but he says he knows I'm good for it and can wait till your money comes in. In the meantime, Mim has been driving all the way from Topsail and picking me up for school. I know it's a long way out of her way, but she lives closer than anyone else at Miller Motte. I told her that when your pay came in, I would give her some money for gas.

Mr. Bolton came by too. I showed him the newest leak in the upstairs. It's in the bathroom this time. You know, he's pretty good about checking up on things here at the house. And he hasn't mentioned a thing about paying him for anything. He's a nice old man. He said he'd be around next week with his ladder and he'd climb on the roof and patch it. I know you'd do that if you were here, but you're not. You're in sunny Vietnam, thinking about me and how beautiful I am and how much you miss me. Ha ha.

Naomi drew a heart after the last sentence and added, *I sure do miss you. I think of you all the time and sometimes wish I had not started on the pill and that I had a little Roy to keep me company. But I guess it is all for the best, since I have to go to school and work. The Riverview is busy on weekends. I make pretty good on tips. I made ten dollars last weekend. That's really good, but then we were really busy. I'm hoping that Mr. Guy has my car ready this weekend so I don't miss work and can start driving myself to Miller Motte.*

Mr. Bolton said he would give me a ride to the restaurant if the car isn't ready. I guess I could use the boat to go to work, but you know me, I'm not very good with starting the motor. Ha ha.

See, you don't need to worry about me at all. I've got everything under control.

Only thing, I try not to miss you so much at night. I miss your touching me and kissing me and the way….

Naomi giggled as she wrote. Imagining how the words and suggestive writing would affect her husband, she embellished, adding oohs and aahs, accentuating the softness of her hair after she shampooed and dried it, comparing it to their nights of passion. She knew, as he had stated in earlier letters, that when he closed his eyes, he could almost smell her and feel her softness.

CHAPTER 4

Naomi stepped into the sunlit morning and walked to the mailbox by the road. Reaching in, she pulled out two letters, both in the familiar red and blue edged envelopes. Her heartbeat quickened as she felt the ambivalent pulses of joy and fear wrestling in her mind. She glanced at her watch; she had about thirty minutes before Norwood Bolton would be there to pick her up for work. Settling herself in one of the rocking chairs on the porch, she pulled one of the two letters she'd received from Roy from her pocket. Feeling it with her fingers, Naomi caressed the letter, held it to her heart for a moment then opened it.

Hey baby, it began, *been busy, thinking of you. Just got back from a mission, the sky was beautiful, lots of clouds. Not much time to write, but I wanted to drop you a line and tell you I love you.*

Love and more love, Roy

She chuckled, folded it back into the envelope and lifted the other letter from her lap. Again, she felt it between her palms, touched it to her breast and then slowly tore the side edge away. This was a longer letter, three pages, back and front. Naomi inhaled and started.

My love, it began, and then the words poured forth, a jumble of how beautiful the skies were, how the blue matched her eyes. *Are you watching the stars? I look at them I see your smile and eyes and I know you're looking at me. Did you see them Sunday night?* He asked, and then began the spurts of *I don't know, I don't believe, it's not right, it's not going to happen. Son of a bitch. Wish I could come home to you.*

There were no specifics. The letter rambled, vacillating between doubt and surety, between anger and a profundity of what he loved and hated. But there was nothing particular mentioned about where he was or what he was doing.

I do my best for my country, they depend on me. The phrases rambled between loss and accomplishment and fearing that he would lose her love.

Roy's doubt, the language he used was new to Naomi and she felt the threads of cold fear run through her veins. She read the letter again, and again, searching for meaning and for clues.

The letter ended with: *I'm sorry. I just don't know anymore.*

Naomi was well aware of the regulations on correspondence. Roy was even more aware and if he hadn't omitted things, the Navy would have made sure they were blackened out.

Something, and Naomi did not know what, was tearing at the man she loved and all she could do was read the words. She couldn't put her arms around him or whisper sweet, calming words. There was nothing she could do. The pain of that impotence wrestled within her and she called out his name, pulling hope from the air, closing her eyes and praying for God to heal her man, to be with him, to hold him as she would.

Tears fell and streamed down her cheeks and Naomi buried her face in her hands.

"I tell you what now," Mr. Bolton began, as he closed the gate behind him and sauntered into the front yard. He leaned against the front porch banister. "That was some storm we had the other night," Norwood said. He stepped closer and handed Naomi a handkerchief. He studied the young woman's face as he reached a hand to pat her hair. "Now, now, there little gal, you don't want to look all teary when I take you to work, do you?" He was silent for the while it took Naomi to compose herself. "Wasn't expecting that little storm to be so bad, blew the bimini right off my boat, got a tear in it. You up to sewing?" He nodded as he followed Naomi's gesture to join her in the rocking chairs on the porch.

"I've never sewn a bimini, but I guess it isn't much different than a shirt or dress. I'll give it a try."

Sitting, he nodded a thank you and asked, "You fare okay over here during that storm? How's that hole in the bathroom, the leak? I know I've been promising to get over and fix it. Well, here I am. Soon as I get back from dropping you off at the Riverview, I'm back here. Got my ladder and everything." Norwood nodded toward his truck parked across the road as his broad face beamed a toothy smile; his green eyes squinted against the sun as he raised his hat to wipe the sweat from his balding pate. "Kinda warm for October, don't ya think?"

Naomi nodded and, lowering her eyes for a moment, stuffed the letters into her pocket.

"You're going to be really glad you two decided to buy this place, once I get it fixed up for you." His eyes raised to the roof of the two-story house and then slid to the far window on the corner. "Yeah, I'll take a look at that window too. By the time Roy gets back from overseas, everything'll l be fixed."

"That cat was over here during the rainstorm, caterwauling to beat all. I don't think the woman that owns him feeds it or takes care of him at all."

Naomi blew her nose in the handkerchief she held balled in her hand.

"I don't really think that woman even owns it." He leaned in. "You're talking about Miss Emmy over across the way?" He pointed to the house beyond the empty lots."

Naomi nodded.

His grin broadened as he began, "Funny thing about that cat, I don't think anybody owns him, he hangs around where he can get some food."

"I've seen her feed him, so…."

"Well, you ain't gonna believe me, but that cat has been caterwauling around here since I was a boy, same black cat with the same glazed eye."

Naomi laughed and wiped her eyes again. "You're full of baloney, Mr. Norwood. That cat isn't fifty years old." She laughed again.

"I'm telling you all I know, that cat's been meowing forever and with the same glazed eye. Story goes that it was hanging around the boats back in the 20s and got it caught in a hook when he tried to steal a fish." His eyes slid to meet hers; his crooked smile broadened and he winked.

Naomi liked Mr. Bolton. He always made her laugh--made her get her mind off of any sadness she felt about Roy. She pulled the envelopes from her pocket, held them in her lap and began, "I got a letter … it makes no sense Mr. Bolton, I'm worried. What do I do?"

"You call me Norwood, my wife does, everybody does." He chuckled as he took the letter from Naomi's outstretched hand. His thumb gently pulled the flap open. Unfolding the pages, Norwood ceased rocking as his eyes perused the writing.

Still softly rocking, Naomi watched his eyes narrow, his mouth purse. She sighed heavily, her hand holding tightly to the arm rests.

He never said a thing as he read, but as his eyes lifted from the last page, Norwood shook his head.

"What do you think?" Naomi asked.

"Something happened to shake him up."

"What?"

"I can no more answer that than the man in the moon."

"Something isn't right is it, Mr. Norwood?"

"Nothing's right when you're in a war, sugar pie." Reaching his hand to pat Naomi's head again, he rose from the chair. "The only thing you can do is write back how much you love him, don't ask questions, because whatever it is, he can't answer you. Don't mention that you're worried or anything, just keep telling him about how much you miss him and that you're busy with … school and work and maybe that you go to the beach and it reminds you of him."

"It's hard."

Patting her head, flattening somewhat her teased hairstyle, Norwood added, "Best thing you can do is think about good stuff, and ...." He reached into the pocket of his worn trousers, and extended his flattened palm. In the center lay a pendant about the size of a half dollar. The brassy metal twined around itself, revealing bits of purple stone.

"How pretty, it looks like wisteria." Naomi reached to touch the pendant and asked, "Did you make this?"

"Take it," he pushed his hand nearer.

"What is it?"

"Take it. This will protect you and give you powers to ward of that old mother-in-law of yours and will help protect Roy."

She fought to keep from rolling her eyes. "Oh, I couldn't take it Mr. Norwood. I ... I don't really believe ...."

He laughed, "Of course you don't, but I do. Now, you take this and wear it or keep it in your handbag or ...." Norwood grinned, touched the fingers of his left hand over the stone and closed his eyes, then opened them and added, "This is simply a good luck charm. It represents beauty, self-healing and wisdom. It's strong in the powers of prosperity and longevity." He paused, cocked his head to the side and pushed his palm forward a bit more. "Take it, hold it every night, think of your husband, believe in it and in him." Norwood chuckled, "And just before his momma comes calling, you stroke this piece and think of how you're going to put her in her place."

Naomi reached to take the pendant, and she held it in her fingers. They closed around it and she could have sworn she felt warmth emanate from it. Her eyes widened as she looked into Norwood's.

"Getting warm, ain't it?" His gap-toothed grin widened.

She nodded, not believing, yet stunned that the thing she held in her hand felt different.

"Don't dwell on the bad stuff or worry about things. He nodded to her still-closed hand. "Just keep this thing with you … hmm, you say that cat's been coming around meowing?"

"Yes sir."

"That's good. That cat, I'm telling you little missy, has got the power too. It comes around you because it likes you. Be nice to him, he'll keep you safe." Norwood's eyes brightened a bit. "You go and have fun, don't sit around here moping and worrying. You enjoy life, but not too much." He winked. "Go with your girlfriends, go dancing, enjoy your life. Maybe go play some putt-putt on Peru road. That's always fun and it's not too far."

Bolton pulled a pipe from his shirt pocket and lit it against the breeze. "Well, little lady, if you don't want to be late for work, we better get going."

Naomi rose, stuffed the letters back into her purse and the pendant into her pocket. She didn't know what to think. If she gave the gift back, she would insult her landlord, and she didn't want to do

46

that. Naomi liked Norwood. He watched out for her and repaired the house when needed, but this hocus pocus stuff was weird.

Feeling uneasy as they drove to the Riverview Restaurant, Naomi reached her hand into her pocket and touched the pendant. With all the twining and small stones, it was still smooth, flowing, one branch to another that led to the clusters of stones that hung likes grape, like wisteria. She could almost smell the thick, sweet scent of the flowers.

Her home, the one she had grown up in at Sloop Point, had two wisteria trees. Actually, they had taken over the big oak near the house and one of the cypress trees near the pond. Her mother was forever pruning the one by the house. When in season, her home smelled like a flower garden.

Naomi's thoughts wandered about her old home until she saw the front of the Riverview. "Oh, I'm sorry Mr. Norwood, but I forgot to ask you if you would check on my car at Guy's Garage, to see if they have my car fixed yet. Could you do that please?"

Sucking from the pipe, he blew a plume of cherry-smelling smoke from the window. "Yes ma'am, I'll do that. I'll be on that roof most of the day. I'll see if Mary can bring over the bimini for you to sew." His eyes squinted against the sun and he added, "You hold on to that little thing I gave you, you hear?"

* * * *

Mary slid close to her husband as Naomi squeezed into the front seat of the truck. In her lap she held the folded bimini, the one Norwood had mentioned earlier that day. Turning to face Naomi, Mary smiled softly. "Norwood told me about the letter."

Naomi tensed for a moment, wishing he hadn't.

"Don't worry little gal," she patted Naomi's thigh. "I understand."

"I tell Mary everything," Norwood began. "If you don't want her to know, don't tell me. But don't you worry. Mary's good as gold, nothing you say to her ever goes any further. Like Andy Griffith says on his show, tick a lock."

Mary pressed two fingers to her lips and twisted them. "Tick a lock," she echoed. "And he told me about the wisteria he gave you." She winked. "It works, Naomi. You just have to believe."

"Yes ma'am. I'll try." Her eyes studied the houses as they passed, most with boats and nets laid out in the yards. She only partly listened to Norwood and Mary's comments on how they remembered how things were when they were young and when he was away in Europe during World War II.

"He was over there in Europe," Mary began, "and I was home up in Beaufort with my family and we were married and I was pregnant. Lost that baby. The only one we ever had. I couldn't wait to get over her on my own. It was hard times with his mom and dad, they never liked me." Mary chuckled. "But I tell you I missed Norwood more than I disliked them. I had this painted rock I used to hold… it was like your wisteria, I guess. I remember once when I was sitting on the couch and …."

Naomi half listened as Mary went on with her story. Half of her wished she cared enough to listen and the other half wished she had never shown Norwood the letters. Mostly, she wished she could go back to feeling comfortable about the couple, like before, when they'd seemed like such friendly, normal folks and not so strange.

"Those were tough times," she heard Norwood say.

Mary echoed him. "Tough times."

"We didn't have it like you have now. No television."

"No television," Mary repeated.

"And the only way to hear about what was going on in the world was on newsreels in the movies. And what the newspapers said, and on the radio," Norwood said. "But that would be days after things happened, sometimes weeks."

"Usually weeks," Mary stressed. "We had to cut back on everything. But when I came over here to live, I had plenty to eat, fish and shellfish. I had a little garden. I didn't need much with Norwood being away, there was only me." She patted Naomi again. "Kinda like you, little gal."

It was nearly dark as they drove in front of her home. Naomi set her hand on the door handle, ready to go inside, to relax and rest her feet, but she heard the other door handle and watched as Mary slid out of the driver's side door with her husband, still holding the bimini top.

"I'll just take this in for you. Besides, I'd like to talk to you a little. Reassure you about things. You know, Roy has it so much easier than Norwood did. He was on the ground. He fought in Okinawa and Iwo Jima. He saw really bad things. And I know he hasn't told me all of it."

"Never will," muttered Norwood. "The past is dead and gone."

Naomi pushed the door open, confused, trying to be polite, wanting so much for them to leave.

"I'm just going to go in and make some coffee, ok?" Mary plopped the bimini on a chair and made her way to the kitchen.

"I'm going to check on the bathroom upstairs where the hole is at," Norwood called from the stairway. "Patched the roof, I need to take a look at what needs to be done inside."

Alone for what Naomi knew would only be moments, she fell onto the edge of the sofa and propped her feet up on the hassock. Reaching into the pocket of her apron, she pulled out a handful of coins. She spread them out on the table and spied the pendant. It was still there. But then, there was no need for it not to be. On and off during the day she had felt for it in the pocket. She shook her head, annoyed and confused about the couple and their gift, their *words of wisdom*.

Pushing the pendant aside, she separated the coins into groups of nickels, dimes and quarters. Someone had left her a dollar. That was rare. Most left change. But tips had been good that day. Not as good as some Saturdays, but still good enough. The eleven-to-seven shift should have yielded more, since she had worked lunch and dinner. *I probably wasn't as attentive as I should have been,* she thought as she counted the coins.

Hearing the clink of cups and saucers, she quickly scooped the coins into her purse.

"How you like it?" Mary called from the kitchen.

"Cream and two sugars," Naomi called back.

Norwood was making his way back down the stairs and both he and Mary reached the living room at the same time, each settling themselves in chairs on either side of her.

Mary leaned forward again and placed her hand on Naomi's knee. "We don't want you to worry about a thing, you hear?"

Norwood scooted closer too. "We're gonna watch out for you, okay?"

"I'm fine, really," Naomi offered.

"Now you listen here, little gal, I saw you this morning and you were a mess."

"He said you were a fright, Naomi. Now don't try to hide things, I mean, unless you don't want us to know. We surely do not want to be where we're not wanted or stick our noses where we shouldn't."

Naomi nodded, stunned by all the attention. Careful not to say something that may be taken wrong, she patted the hands still resting near her. "I'm fine, really. You caught me at a bad time this morning, Mr. Norwood. That's all."

He leaned back, studying her, folding his hands across his stomach.

Mary mimicked him, except her hands lay folded in her lap. "Don't try to suppress it, dearie. Let it out. I know I used to cry my eyes out just about every day."

Norwood leaned forward. "Let me tell you a little story, little gal. Talk about life being hard, let me tell you about people and lies and death and...."

Mary nodded her head fervently. "He's telling you the truth. Tell her Nor, tell her about that woman and all she caused you." She turned to

Naomi, "And this was before he ever went in the service. Go on now, Nor, tell her, tell her."

Norwood spread his arms on the chair rests, took a deep breath and began, "Well, like I was saying, there was this woman, felt sorry for her." He nodded to Mary. "We both did. She was renting from my family. I hate to call her a damn Yankee, 'cause I have friends that come from up north that are just as fine a folks as can be, but this damn woman beat all. Now, she could peal the paint right off the side of your house, making you think she was smart as a whip and honest as the day is long, but ... she sure had me fooled, she had everybody fooled and I was just a kid back then.

"Her name was Abby, and she was from Connecticut, I think, or maybe Vermont, I don't know, but she had me fooled and good, at least in the beginning. You see, my momma had gotten hurt helping Daddy, trying to save him. For weeks, maybe even months, Momma was just lost. Yeah, she missed my daddy and it took something out of her, but she wasn't stupid." Norwood slid his eyes to meet Naomi's. He pursed his mouth around the pipe he held between his teeth for a moment, then began again. "But that damn Abby, well, she treated my poor old momma like she didn't have no brains at all." He slid his eyes back again, raising a brow this time and added, "Yep, them damn Yankees think we're all dumb as tires down here. Everything they do is better, we don't know a damn thing, well, you tell me where all the riots are and all the slums, ain't down here."

He stopped for a moment and shrugged, then continued on, "Abby would go on and on about how she'd been taking care of her aunts and her own momma and she knew how to take care of people and how she respected the old folks. Well, Momma wasn't that old then, she was only in her fifties, but I think Daddy's dying aged her twenty years. Her hair started getting grayer and her shoulders started slumping. Good lord, Miss Naomi, she was pulling in them traps and throwing 'em out right alongside my daddy when he was living. She was strong as an ox and she put up with my daddy and us kids, and on top of that she kept the books for the church and read at least two books a week. My momma was smart, I tell you." His eyes widened as they stared into Naomi's.

"So, she was your mother's housekeeper, after your daddy died, this Abby?" Naomi queried, still somewhat confused by the story.

"Yeah, well, she was more than that. She cooked and helped my momma clean up herself and drove her to the store." He shook his head. "Poor old Momma wasn't herself after Daddy died. She saw it happen, you see, saw him drown, even jumped in the water and tried to save him. She just couldn't cope with it, him drowning, not being able to save him. It was too much for her … for a while, then … well, I'll get to that." Norwood smiled grimly and tapped his pipe on the arm of the rocking chair.

"This Abby woman started working for us, wormed her way right in, cause she and her husband lived right next door. They were renting that little place beside us back then. He had been in the Army, or so Abby said, but he was never home though. I heard Momma tell Daddy a bunch of times that she thought Abby ran out on her husband.

"At least, that was what I heard. But I always felt sorry for her, in the beginning. I did, but then I realized her husband probably had to get away to keep his sanity. Before Daddy's accident, my momma would go over to their house to visit her. She had a two-year-old kid and there'd be dirty diapers thrown in the corner of the room. The place smelled like you-know-what and my momma at first felt sorry for her too, thinking that she had her hands full raising a baby and didn't have time for cleaning. Well, she'd help her clean and then one day, after they'd been renting from us for about a month, she came home, sat down and said that she thought that girl was just plumb lazy, that she didn't really need any help. She said that poor baby was always squalling, and looked sickly and it was because Abby didn't do it right.

"Pitickity was roaming around then, but that cat stayed far away from that house while those people were there," Mary interrupted.

"So you see, Momma knew about Abby," continued Norwood, "about what kind of person she was, and then it wasn't long after that, maybe a few days, that Daddy drowned. And that Abby came over saying that she'd watch my momma since Momma had helped her out so much. What a fool I was, I didn't know what to do. Here my daddy was just dead and my momma couldn't even talk hardly, so I took it like it was supposed to be. You see, I was only about fourteen or fifteen."

Norwood's eyes glanced sadly at Naomi and looked quickly away. He shrugged. "That's life, I suppose, you never know what you're gonna get."

"Did she hurt your momma or steal anything from your family?" Naomi asked, her hand holding her chin as she leaned forward and took a sip from the coffee.

"She drove Momma to the doctor, the head doctor, what they call a shrink now, and Momma got on some pills for a while that were supposed to keep her from being so depressed. But I never did think they did her any good. I always thought they made it worse for her. She started staring at the walls a lot. She was drooling, and she'd sit and talk to herself and that damn Abby would drive her to the doctor and get more pills and then one day my neighbor, Doris Wells, on the other side of me, the little yellow house, said she saw her push my mother into the car. She was talking mean to her and then when Doris walked up to her, Abby started threatening her, saying that she was going to call the police on her for running into the mailbox." Norwood leaned in. "She did run into the mailbox, and then Abby threatened her saying she was going to tell the police how her kids were always picking the roses off of my mother's bush. Well, I know my mother knew that, so did Daddy, when he was alive, but they never did mind.

"This had been going on for a few months and no telling what Abby was telling the doctor. Then Aunt Helen came for a visit, down from West Virginia and the poop hit the propeller." Norwood laughed aloud. "She went in to the doctor when Abby was there with Momma and I tell you what, things changed after that. Even though that Abby woman came knocking on the door and told Aunt Helen that she was going to sue her for slander. Aunt Helen told her she was lucky that she didn't end up in jail for all the lying to the doctor and the over-medication on Momma and that was the last we saw of that bag of worms. She took herself and her two-year-old baby and was gone in two days."

"What about her husband?"

Norwood shrugged, "If he was smart, he stayed as far away from that trouble-making hussy as he could."

"You know a lot of strange people don't you, Mr. Norwood?"

He smiled sheepishly. "Takes all kinds. Just remember, don't trust anybody. People will fool you. It might be money is their weakness, or maybe it's power, or control. It can be any number of *things* that turns a man into a liar or manipulator, but if you know someone and they got a *thing*, get as far away from them as possible." He eyed the pendant still on the end table next to Naomi. "But that, that ain't no *thing*, that's real. You just have to believe."

"Just believe," mimicked Mary.

The lines of her brow drawn together, Naomi nodded her head. "You're right, you sure are right. I know somebody just like Abby--charm the scales right off a snake."

Norwood smiled and raised a brow. "Comes visiting around once a month, huh? Your mother-in-law, Mrs. Lenore Simpson, right?"

Naomi laughed. "Yep."

"But you just hold that wisteria talis I gave you and all that will change."

"Okay." Naomi winked; it was best to humor them than to confess how she truly felt about the token.

Norwood winked back. "Now, you don't worry about that letter either, you hear?"

Naomi shrugged, lowered her eyes and sucking in her bottom lip, then nodded her head. Her eyes burned. "Okay." Looking up to meet Norwood's sympathetic eyes, she whispered, "I'll be fine."

Mary crossed her legs and sipped from the coffee. "Everybody has a life. You make the best of yours. You wait and see, things will work out, just believe."

Norwood nodded. "Fubar."

"What! What do you mean *fubar*? This is serious, it's not ... you know."

"I'm saying, more than likely, what's in that letter is fubar. Everything is fubar in a war."

Holding her hands over her eyes, Naomi shook her head. It was just getting too weird now. "What does fubar mean?" she cautiously asked.

"Old military term," he chuckled. "Right popular term during WWII."

"Oh." Naomi was afraid to ask what, fearing it might lead to another strange story.

"You're going to have to have Mary tell you about it sometime. It's not something I like talking about but I can tell you one thing, I know when I came up and saw you with your head in your hands that it was Vietnam, the war." He winked. "Fubar, it's all fubar. That damn President Johnson doesn't know what he's doing. He got us into this thing now."

Her lips trembled again and Norwood chuckled. "Little gal, your man is the safest place he could be, up in the air. I was a grunt, a Marine grunt, the pointy end of the stick. Be glad your man ain't no grunt." Standing, he held a hand to help her up. "Now, we better get going, and if I ain't mistaken, I think you think we talk too much. I think you think we're a bit on the spooky side with all the talk about wisteria and powers." Norwood didn't laugh this time. "Next week we'll bring around the sacrificial lamb."

Her mouth dropped again and Naomi held out her hand as if to stop traffic. "Oh no, I can't..."

Mary and Norwood burst out laughing.

"Sacrificial lamb, you hear that, Mary? She thinks I'm serious."

Naomi laughed with them, not sure if they were serious or not. Unsure about the pendant and the powers the couple swore by. Laughing nervously, she thanked them for the ride, for fixing the roof and for their time. At the door she hugged each one and waved good-bye as they drove away.

She was glad when they were finally gone. Naomi wanted time to be alone, to think, to drink in all that had happened that day. She slinked onto the sofa, pulling her feet up and laying her head on the rest. She wanted to laugh about the stories and advice the Boltons had given her. She smiled and thought of the things they'd said that made sense and of the things that didn't. "Sure are strange," she muttered. She glimpsed the pendant and thought of the cat. Certainly, Pitickity had not been around for fifty years and certainly the wisteria pendant held no powers either.

She thought of writing to Roy about these things, but quickly disregarded the idea. Mentioning them might only make him worry and he needed to worry just about as much as she needed to.

Part of her was glad Norwood and Mary were in her life. They surely offered more caring and understanding than her own parents. Maybe it was all a joke, maybe they were playing a joke on her with the pendant and the cat. But she didn't want to think about that now, she didn't want to dissect what meant what. She laughed at herself for a moment, as her mind wandered to the possibility that the pendant might work on her mother-in-law. "That would be nice," she said aloud. "The old witch would fit right in with that kind of hocus pocus."

She sighed, thinking of the Boltons again and, walking up the stairs to go to her bed, she dismissed the bizarre suggestions and thought of how nice it was to have friends who cared about her, even if they were kind of weird.

Maybe it's because they never had children. Maybe with all the time on their hands they find things to entertain them, odd things, but maybe they like me and so what if they're weird? If they want to treat me like I'm their surrogate daughter and offer advice and help me, that's okay with me.

"I'll be their surrogate daughter, since my own parents have their asses on their shoulders." Naomi thumbed her chin. "Serves them right, if they can't accept me like I am and so what if I didn't go to the University of North Carolina? I'm married to the best man in the whole world and I'm going to Miller Motte and I'm going on my own dime."

Smiling, relaxing to feelings of security and accomplishment, Naomi fell asleep, but only for a few moments before the sharp rap on the door.

"Hey, open up princess." The knocking was louder this time. "I'm all dressed and ready."

Naomi roused from her moments-long nap and opened the door to Vickie, her long, blonde hair capped with a witch's hat, her body clothed in the black garb of a witch. Smiling at Naomi, she crinkled and twitched her nose.

"I'm Samantha, don't you recognize me?" Vickie held her wand up and out to her side as she twirled. "How do I look?"

"Great, I'd recognize you anywhere."

"Looks like I woke you up. Don't tell me you're not ready?" Tapping Naomi lightly with the wand, Vickie cooed, "You're wide awake now and ready to go get dressed and party."

"Oh no, not tonight. I'm so tired and isn't it kind of late?" Bending her body to look beyond the door, Naomi asked, "Where are the kids?"

"Oh, they're in bed. I already took the kids trick-or-treating earlier." Vickie pushed past Naomi into the living room. "Come on now, it's eight-thirty, the party is starting, and you promised."

"I thought we were taking the kids trick-or-treating."

"Silly rabbit, trick-or-treating is for kids," Vickie tittered. "We're going to a real *adult* Halloween party. Get your costume on. What are you dressing as?"

"I don't want …."

"Well, you are. You promised and I got a baby sitter and everything and so you're going." Vickie grabbed Naomi by the arm. "Come on now. Up the stairs we go to see what you have in your pretty closet full of pretty things. I know you have them."

Twenty minutes later, Naomi stood in front of the full-length mirror. On her head was a crown of plastic pink roses, on her feet were a pair of fluffy black bedroom slippers. She wore a smokey gray dress and a lavender ribbon around her neck. Covering the tea-length dress was the lavender dressing gown she had purchased the last time Roy had been home. It hung loosely over the gray dress and just below its hem line.

Naomi had found her eye-liner and shadow and applied them liberally to her eyes and added only a touch of rouge to her cheeks and lips.

Teasing her friend's thick hair higher, Vickie exclaimed, "You look witchy, like Endora on *Bewitched*. You know, the TV show. Oh, and you need a clip or tiara in your hair like Endora wears too."

Naomi pulled out a drawer to her vanity. Inside were what seemed dozens of hair bows and clips.

"No tiara, no queen for a day tiara?" Vickie laughed aloud and picked a long, flat clip studded with purple beads to fasten into Naomi's hair. She peered for a moment in the mirror at her friend. "And you have to have a mole on the side of your cheek, and more rouge."

Vickie pressed an eyebrow pencil low on to Naomi's cheek. She pricked her friend's hair out and higher still with her fingertips. "Yep, you look witchy, *we* look witchy, just like Samantha and Endora. Now, let's go."

As they descended the stairs, Naomi spotted the purple and brass pendant on the end table and, grabbing a ribbon, tied it around her neck. "This does it, don't you think? Just like Endora."

Her fingers touching the pendant, Vickie caught her breath. "Wisteria. I always liked wisteria, but it is a kind of spooky plant, don't you think? It grows like crazy and takes over everything, just like a witch's fingers. Stretching her fingers, long fake nails extended, she cackled loudly, "and now my pretty!"

"Are we doing the *Wizard of Oz* or *Bewitched*?"

CHAPTER 5

"Where in the heck is this party at?" Naomi asked as Vickie pulled through the old brick pillars that once stood as the entrance to Camp Davis in Holly Ridge.

"Way down here, there's an old building, used to be a fire house or something. Anyway, Danny and me and a few others have been over here today fixing it up. It's spooky as hell. We have fake spider webs and skeletons and even a goblin that glows." Vickie cackled, witch-like, and arched her back. "It looks so hip, Naomi. The house is covered in old dead vines and there's a couple of trees without leaves and we put paper ghosts on it and Jimmy got a black light. It looks really freaky."

It had been ages since Naomi had been to a party without Roy. It felt odd and she wondered if it would be like it used to, herself the belle of the ball. Raising a brow, she sneered and thought how unlikely that would be now, with things having changed so in the last few years.

"Anybody bring some Jack Daniels or beer?" she asked. "I could probably use a drink."

"I'm sure there's something. Ted Langly is supposed to be here and you know he's never without." Vickie patted Naomi's hand. "What's up? You feeling a little nervous?"

"It's been a while since I've been out or done anything except work. Roy's not here and I feel sort of naked without him."

"Oh, hang loose, sugar. You'll be fine. You're among friends. People who have known you since diapers."

The car bumped along the old, abandoned roads that were once part of the World War Two camp. Even in the dimming light of day, Naomi could see the discarded beer cans and old paper cups alongside the roads. She didn't want to be reminded of where her husband was. She didn't want to go to a place where, more than likely, the attendants would be kids that would judge her, and of course they would ask about Roy and Vietnam.

Closing her eyes, she reminded herself that all she had to do was pretend, pretend that everything was all right, that her life was going as planned, that all was well with Roy and that he was safe. She touched the wisteria pendant around her neck, smiled and then giggled. *Thank God for the Boltons.*

Naomi concentrated on Roy's last visit. It had been wonderful; he hadn't talked of how bad it was or about buddies being killed or anything about what some of the newsmen on television were saying. She hadn't asked. Roy was strong, he was himself and was proud to be a Navy pilot and bombardier with ten kills flying the F-4 Phantom. She was his rock, and he was hers.

Vickie's Volkswagen Beetle came to a stop, jolting Naomi from the images of her husband. Lifting her eyes to her surroundings, she had to admit that whomever had decorated the building had done a perfect job. It did look spooky with the aging vines covering the abandoned structure, a few windows broken out and hand-carved jack-o-lanterns with burning candles sitting in the windows. In the yard, she noticed the trees Vickie had mentioned, covered in sheet "ghosts" that swayed, dreamlike, in the soft night air.

Long strands of Spanish moss hung from them as well, though she was sure the moss had been there naturally. Somebody had ridden a horse to the occasion and it stood tied to a far oak, without a saddle. She wondered who there had ridden bareback. It prompted a memory of the time she and Roy had taken her family's horses to Topsail and had ridden, lumbering up and down the dunes and splashing through the incoming tide. *Maybe this will be fun*, she thought, and she stepped from the Beetle and toward the house.

"Beach Boys?" she asked herself as she heard the words to one song she often listened to on the radio. Yes, it was them, she realized. She smiled, then laughed aloud as a couple came through the door, one dressed as Cousin It, the other as Morticia from the television show *The Addams Family*.

Loud Music filtered from inside into the night air, bringing with it the smell of cigarette smoke and laughter; Naomi walked inside, not hesitant in the least as she heard her name called. She looked to see classmates from Topsail school, whom she had not seen since graduation. And, though it had only been five years, it seemed a lifetime as she greeted former cheerleaders and glee club participants.

There was an *I Dream of Jeanie* Jeanie, another Cousin It, two Lily Munsters, Herman Munster, a Gomez Addams, Ginger from *Gilligan's Island*, two or three Gilligans, and countless others dressed as the popular TV stars of the day. One guy had come dressed as Spock from the television show *Star Trek*. He had the pointy ears and everything; Naomi recognized him as the kid in biology who sat behind her. She nodded a hello, and he nodded back.

She recognized another Endora and Samantha as students she'd seen in school, though she could not recall their names, but it seemed they had all been friends back then, or at least liked each other.

Lacing her arm through Naomi's, Vickie handed her friend a tall glass of something pink with a twist of lemon peel on the rim. "Here, taste this, you'll like it."

"Oh, I don't…"

"Just a touch of rum in some Hawaiian Punch and Seven Up, try it."

Naomi sipped. It was sweet, but not too sweet and she could barely taste the rum.

"The guys are swilling beer, but Dotty made up a pitcher of this for us girls. I don't like beer either."

"It's good," Naomi cooed, "but only one, I have to work tomorrow."

Lacing her arm through Naomi's again, Vickie led the way to a small group of people gathered around a table. "Hey, you remember Carl and Betty and Debbie and Linda?" She bumped a bearded young man. "And Arthur, you remember him, don't you?"

Naomi did, she remembered them all, but it seemed so long ago and she had seen none of them except for Vickie since graduation. Back then, her whole world had been Roy; her classmates had barely existed. Honestly, she felt as if she did not know them at all any longer. Most of them had gone to college and she had gone to Sneads Ferry.

Her eyes wandered the room as the others exchanged remembrances, and she caught the gaze of the kid dressed as Spock from *Star Trek*. He nodded and smiled, then laughed a bit. Raising his highball glass high he mimicked a toast, then drank from it.

Naomi moved closer to him, trying to remember just how well she had known him in school.

"I remember you. You sat in front of me in science," the young man spoke sarcastically.

She nodded, suddenly remembering how she'd never felt good around *Elmo*. The name came instantly to her as he spoke. Wasn't he the one who always added the phrase *like a race car* to the end of other people's sentences? Naomi recalled the time he had brought a huge moth to school in a jar and then lit it on fire in Biology class. *He always gave me the heebie jeebies,* she thought as she feigned a smile, regretting immediately that she had moved toward him. She took another sip from the punch and asked, "What have you been up to since we were at Topsail?

"I graduated from Berkeley last year."

"Oh, that's nice." She moved to turn away and Elmo touched her arm. "I have a degree in Psychology, got my minor in Chemistry," he nodded. "You look wonderful, haven't changed a bit. I bet you're still as popular as ever, huh?"

"Isn't Berkeley in California?" Naomi ignored the remark.

Elmo chuckled, closing his eyes. His lips twisting into a smirk. "Of course, Berkeley is in California. It's the hippest place to be." He sipped form the highball glass in his hand. "I can't believe I grew up here. Things are so hip in California, it's like I grew up in the stone age here." His hooded eyes scanned her body and he laughed gently. "Endora, I get it, groovy. You could be her, you know. Are you going to put a spell on me?"

She half-laughed and looked around the room, hoping to find someone to wave to or some way of getting away from Elmo.

"I got a job in Charlotte ...."

Naomi nodded, "That's good."

"I'm thinking of going to Chapel Hill and getting a doctorate."

She nodded again.

"I'm just here visiting my aunt Karen. Just thought I'd see how the gang was doing."

What gang could he be talking about? Naomi thought. *Elmo never hung out with anyone.* She sipped the remainder of the punch from her glass.

"Here," Elmo offered, "let me get a refill for you."

"No, don't bother--"

"One more isn't going to hurt, now." He walked briskly away as Naomi scanned the room, searching for another familiar face, any excuse to leave where she was now standing. Finally, she caught the eye of a familiar girl from Glee Club. She waved, and the girl waved back.

"Going? Elmo asked, returning with the refilled glass. Lifting his head to notice the girl from Glee Club, he chuckled. "Myrna, I remember her too. Neither one of you would ever give me the time of day, back then."

You gave me the creeps, creep. Naomi's eyes met Elmo's and quickly turned away.

"Drink up, hot stuff, this is like the best drink you will ever have. It will take you places."

Naomi smirked, Elmo winked and watched as she took a long sip from the glass. She smiled and shrugged. "Do you mind if I talk with Myrna?"

"Bummer, yeah, you hang loose." He nodded, snickered and added. "Enjoy the trip! It's like a race car."

What in the hell does he mean by that? Naomi sipped generously from the drink as she moved toward Myrna. Holding the glass in her hand, she swirled it a bit before taking another sip. "Hi Myrna, been a long time," she began.

Myrna, rolled her eyes, "Still the same creep, huh?"

"Yep."

"Do you remember the thing about the moth in Biology?"

"Yeah," Naomi rolled her eyes again. He burned it while it was still alive.

"Once a creep, always a creep."

Naomi nodded. "I love the costume, Ginger, right? You look just like her--love the hair and let me hear you talk like her."

Myrna giggled then began, softening her voice to sound sexy. "Ooh Gilligan, you're so sweet."

"That's it! You sound just like her."

"I love your costume too, Naomi. I bet you made it yourself, didn't you? You were always so good in Home Economics."

"Pretty good huh?" Naomi giggled as she sipped from her glass. "I can hardly taste the rum." Tilting the glass to her lips, Naomi glimpsed Elmo standing just beyond the doorway. His fingers making the peace sign, he mouthed something she could not make out and then it occurred to her: *like a race car.*

"Again?" she shook her head and swallowed the rest of her drink.

"What?" echoed Myrna.

"Oh, it's just that Elmo, being ... stupid."

"Oh, he was always odd. I wonder who invited him tonight. He never hung out with any of us." Tilting her head back, Myrna emptied her glass. "Another?"

"No, thank you, I think that was my last." Naomi looked around the room again. Vickie was waving to her and motioning for her to come outside, so Naomi did.

"I saw you talking to Elmo, I just saw him leave. What was he doing here?"

"I have no idea, just bragging about going to college in California." Naomi breathed in the cool October air. It felt good, and despite having just spent fifteen minutes with someone she did not like, she felt good. It was nice to get away from her hum drum life for at least a little while. The party had taken her mind off worrying so much about Roy and made her think of fun days when life was not so complicated.

She looked skywards, to the full moon brightening up the night sky. The clouds hung low and puffy. Looking for the Cassiopeia, Naomi scrunched her brow as a cloud floated in front of the stars, obscuring the constellation. Stretching her neck back, she watched the cloud wisp and swirl, forming letters. Her eyes moved to another cloud and another, wispy and swirling even more. Stepping back, she could see the whole sky, lit by a full moon, and it all looked so amazing. Then by magic, it seemed, the clouds moved into different forms as if being controlled by a paint brush and formed into words: *peace, love, sex*. The words danced there in the night sky, billowy and free, stating, to Naomi, the truth. *The truth shall set you free*. Naomi licked her lips and smiled. *How wonderful to see the words,* she thought.

The breeze was caressing her now, its coolness transitioning to cocoon like warmth. She felt warm and protected, feeling Roy's arms on her body, his touch more electric than ever before. Naomi felt as if she could fly if she desired to, yes, she could fly to Roy. Looking up into the sky, she heard the juddering sound of helicopters.

At first, the idea that she could be with the choppers so high in the sky entered her brain but then a cat's caterwauling broke into her thoughts and her eyes were drawn to the dark colored cat stepping from the side of the building, meowing as it moved close to her. Its eyes shone milky in the glare of the porch lights, and it rubbed against her leg.

****

Vickie lifted the damp cloth from Naomi's forehead, replacing it with another, then pulled the afghan to just below her chin. As Naomi's eyes slowly opened, Vickie asked, "What in the world happened to you? I didn't realize things were so bad."

Her eyes questioning, Naomi shook her head. "What happened?"

"Honey, I've been with you all night. You went bonkers. At the party you were screaming about a devil cat and crying about Roy. And you kept asking me if they were bad. Who? Who did you mean? You kept saying that you had to save Roy, that he was dying and it was the cat's fault. You started running around the yard looking for some damn cat you thought you saw, you said it had evil eyes."

"Me? I don't remember ...." Naomi began as patches of the experience appeared to her.

"You slapped the shit out of Norman. He was just trying to get you into my car so I could take you home. That was the scary part. He had to ride with me to keep you from jumping out of the car, you said some cat was after you."

Naomi's lips were trembling as she pressed her fingers to the sides of her head. "That was so strange, I don't know... why... what ...."

"Norman drove my car back. I wanted to stay-- make sure you were alright."

"What happened?" Naomi repeated. "I remember the party, it was fun, sort of, I guess. Everybody was nice, except ... that guy from science class ... Elmo." Thinking for a moment, Naomi nodded her head. "Yeah, I remember he went and got me another drink, and then he did this thing he used to do in high school."

"What? I know he used to stare at me a lot, creeped me out."

Naomi grimaced. "No, he used to say *like a race car*, or something like that. I didn't know what in the hell he meant then and I don't know now, but as he was leaving, he was standing by the door and he said *like a race car.*" Her mouth pursing, Naomi shut her eyes tight. Holding back tears, she turned her head toward the back of her couch. "I'm sorry. You must think I'm crazy."

"I didn't know what to do." Vickie began, "And I didn't want to call your parents or Roy's. Everyone knows how they feel about you two getting married and then I thought there was a chance that someone put something in the punch, and I waited for a moment for me to flip out, but then Norman said it looked like you were on acid.

"Acid?"

"Oh, come on now, you've heard of that, LSD."

"Oh shit! I don't do drugs, Vickie, you know that."

Nodding, Vickie continued, "Damn Elmo. I bet he spiked your drink."

"Why would he do that?"

"Because he's weird, freaked out. He's always been. As I think about it now, Elmo was not at the party for very long. He left the party just when you went over to talk with Myrna. Yeah, I bet he put something in it. He's been out in California doing all that hippie stuff."

Naomi shifted her body to sit upright. "Do I need to go to a doctor? Am I alright?"

"You tell me, honey. How do you feel? Are you seeing things that aren't there? Do you see any

78

cats?" Vickie reached for the glass on the coffee table. "Here, take a sip of water."

"You sure it's not spiked with anything?" Naomi scowled and added, "I don't think I'll ever drink anything anyone hands me again."

CHAPTER 6

Mim leaned against the headboard of her bed, her knees propped high, the Miller Motte etiquette book leaning against them. The page was turned to a picture of a girl with a book atop her head. The caption read: *Book balancing. Learn to walk gracefully. Walk as if gliding.*

She dog-eared the page and rose from the bed to place the book on her head. With her shoulders pulled back and her hips forward, Mim walked from her bed to the dresser, then to the door and back to her bed. She did this four times, turned her head just slightly to view herself in the mirror and smiled.

A loud rapping and the following *trick or treat!* rang from the living room as Mim plopped the book and herself back on the bed. Exhaling loudly, she found the dog-eared page and flipped to the next. The top of the page read: *Proper weight and height.* Her finger found her height and followed to the pounds she was supposed to weigh.

"Not bad." She thought of the weight she'd lost since starting college. There just didn't seem to be time to eat. Hearing the rapping at the door again, she heard her mother repeat the words. She slammed the book shut and looked at the clock. It was six-thirty. It was Friday night, Halloween Night, and she was at home, not on a date, not at a party.

The only guy she had the slightest interest in was Roger, but she wasn't too sure about that anymore. Yes, she liked him, even cared for him. But things just didn't seem to be moving in the right direction. She'd run into him twice in the last couple of months and they'd exchanged polite hellos. Now, she didn't even want him to ask her out. Now, she felt like a fool and she knew that if she did see him somewhere, she'd run the other way.

A tap on her bedroom door, and Edna opened it softly. "Sweetie, why don't you go to the Kooler and pick us up some ice-cream? I sure would like a banana split."

Mim thought for a moment. She never could refuse her mother's requests, and there had been few.

"My treat, get whatever you want."

Mim thought of a strawberry sundae, then against it. "No, I'm not very hungry, but I'll go get you one." She jumped from the bed, anxious to get out of the house, and pulled on the cardigan draped over the chair to her vanity.

"The kids are out trick-or-treating." Edna held out a bag of popcorn balls she'd made that day. "Here, pass them out if you see any kids. I made so many, too many, I think."

Her mother had always been like that, making too much food, just in case someone dropped by, and as if her husband was still alive. Mim took the bag and kissed Edna on the cheek. "Banana split, huh?"

"Yes, and make sure the banana isn't too ripe."

The screen door slapped gently behind her as Mim walked down the few steps into the front yard. The Kooler, the only place on the island to get soft serve ice cream, was only a block and a half away. She saw a group of kids ahead, a parent guiding them as they moved north toward the Frazier house.

Maybe a couple houses and some visiting fishermen were all I went to when I was a kid, she thought as she neared an empty lot of sand, yucca plants and muhly grass. *There's a few more families on the beach now.* She smiled, watching the children hoot and play in the distance.

The lot was just past her home and catty-corner from the ice cream shop. Her eyes studied the plants there; the muhly grass was in full bloom with its brilliant, soft purple plumage. She thought of picking some for her room for a moment. Instead, she noticed the figure sitting there in the sand alone. Too big to be a child, his head was turned toward her, watching. Mim studied the image for a few moments then turned away, walking faster.

"Hey you," the figure called out.

She quickened her pace.

"Hey, you. Trick or treat."

Mim stopped. She recognized the voice and when she heard the laughter, she knew it was Roger.

"Hey lady, trick or treat," Roger called as he rose and moved toward her.

She wanted to smile as he neared, but didn't.

"What's the matter, no treats for me?" he giggled. "I thought you wanted me to ask you on a date? Well, I'm asking now. Wanna go out with me? Want to go walk on the beach with me?" He laughed again. "Or are you too nice a girl?" Both hands wound round her waist as he pulled her close.

Mim's eyes found his, and she swallowed and backed up a bit. Smelling the air, Mim thought she smelled something odd. Her eyes questioned and Roger spoke. "Wacky tobaccy? Is that it?"

He nodded. "Yes ma'am, guilty as charged." He laughed again.

"But you're a cop."

Roger shrugged. "So, I get the best stuff." Taking her hands in his he asked, "Why don't we go down to the blue house? The time we met there last summer, I really enjoyed that."

Mim stepped back, pulling her hands from his. "Why should I go to the blue house with you?" Her mind flew to the day he'd mentioned, and to Max Burnside, the dead man found there.

Studying Roger's face, Mim felt angry. Who did he think he was, coming up to her after making her feel like such a fool? It had been two months since she had asked him about asking her out. Oh, the twinkle in his eye was charming, and hadn't she wanted this, for him to come to her? Part of her longed for the attention, but another part struggled against it and wanted more cajoling. *Make him ask again*, she thought, and then she smelled the pungent odor of something.

Mim scowled. "I don't like drugs."

Pressing his body against hers, Roger chuckled. "It's not drugs, it's just a little Maryjane, a little Puff the Magic Dragon." His smile was almost irresistible as he spoke. "Isn't this what you want, my arms around you?"

Mim turned her head away from the pungent smell. "What are you doing out here?"

"I'm just enjoying the night ... thinking about you," he smiled sheepishly. "You know what else is Puff the Magic Dragon?"

Staring at him, Mim did not answer.

"Puff the Magic Dragon, like when the AC-47s come, man that is a spooky gunship." Roger tilted his head and drew hard on the joint between his fingers. "When that mother flew by, we knew gooks were going to die. Yeah, Puff the Magic Dragon."

She felt the chill run through her and bit her lip. "I'm sorry."

"What are you sorry about?" He smiled and reached to stroke her cheek. "You are a beautiful girl, a nice girl. Aren't you?"

"I'm sorry you had to go through all that in Vietnam, I guess that is what's the matter with you ...."

"What's the matter with me? What's the matter with you?" Roger chuckled and stepped backward, then reached out his hand to grasp her shoulder, pulling himself close again to her.

"I keep myself away from you, because since I first saw you all I want to do is ...." His lips pressed against her neck, nipping it slightly. He laughed and in a Bela Lugosi accent spoke, "You see, I'm a vampire, I'll suck the life out of you." His laugh was deep, almost sinister and then his eyes searched hers, looking for something, but they were met with nothing he found familiar.

"You don't know me. You don't, do you? You might not really like me, if you did." Studying her face, he spoke again. "You're maybe curious. Maybe want to know how many men I've killed, maybe babies. That's what they call us, that's what they say on the nightly news, that we're baby killers." Roger stepped back. "Okay, good girl. I like you. You go on now and go home." He winked. "But ...." his eyes leered at her body, "I'll see you later." Releasing her, Roger walked slowly across the sandy, empty field.

She watched him make his way along the little path through the yuccas, cactus and stickers and on across the dunes. Standing there, stunned by the encounter, Mim felt her body shaking. Not from fear but from sorrow. Not once had he looked back. Not once had he stopped or paused.

Part of her wanted to go after him, to reassure him that she did not judge him. But she knew she wouldn't do that. Nice girls didn't chase after men.

Feeling the money in her sweater pocket, she thought of her mother and imagined Edna shaking her head no. She could almost hear the words she knew her mother would say: *Best to leave him alone. You don't need any trouble in your life now.* Mim knew that if she told her mother about the encounter, about Roger's behavior, Edna would warn her about the dangers of being involved with a volatile man. Mim thought of Anthony, his anger. How he had turned into someone she didn't recognize. Was it happening again?

The fingers of her hands threaded through her hair and she pulled so slightly. *Is this it? Is this what*

I attract, lonely crazed men? So much of her wanted the soft, loving part of love. She longed for it. *What do I have to do to get that? What part of my soul do I have to sell to get that?*

"Shit." The word burst from Mim's mouth. Confused, she closed the sweater around her and walked to the Kooler. A group of trick-or-treaters were in line ahead of her and she handed the bag of popcorn balls to the one nearest her. "Here, trick or treat. My mother made them."

She heard one of the kids say something about knowing who she was and which house she came from. She heard another one say something about how good the popcorn balls were.

"What will you have? Asked the lady at the window.

Mim ordered her mother's banana split and a strawberry sundae for herself.

CHAPTER 7

There was no need for Mim to drive to Sneads Ferry today; Naomi's car was fixed. And it was nice to get to sleep a little later and take her time about getting ready for the drive to Wilmington. She brushed a mascara wand against her eyelashes and smeared a dab of lipstick on her mouth. Rubbing her lips together, she preened for a few seconds in front of the mirror. She liked the way she looked with less make-up, and with her hair teased less high. She was letting it grow long now and had begun wearing it up. Pulling a few tendrils from the side of her hairdo, she fussed with her hair a little more and then picked up the tiny box of eye shadow. She dabbed just a bit of the blue on the top lid and grabbed her books and purse.

"Bye, Mom!" Mim shouted as she pushed the screen door forward. She stepped onto the front porch and, noticing one of the rockers move, she turned to see Roger.

Holding out a small bouquet of flowers, he said, "I'm sorry about last night."

Mim smiled and took them. "It's okay. I understand."

"I'm sorry if I made you feel foolish and never responded to you asking me out. And last night ... well, I do like you. I like you a lot."

"Me too."

"Gotta go slow, I don't want to mess up a beautiful friendship, not with you."

"Yeah," Mim nodded. "Let's be friends. I like that."

"It's not a good time for me to get really involved, you know, and I spend a lot of time in Jacksonville," his eyes apologized, "on the strip."

Mim knew what he meant and she tried not to judge. "Oh, I see ... maybe you should stop that."

"Yeah ...."

"And you know that marijuana is illegal. For goodness' sake, you're a cop."

"Yeah, I know." Roger leaned against the car and stared at her. "I'm sorry."

"I'm sorry that you had to go to Vietnam."

"I'm not. I'm proud to fight for my country ...." His lips curled for a moment. "And it's just a little grass, it's not bad, Mim."

"It's illegal. You go to jail for that." She stepped toward her car. "I have to go to school, I don't want to be late."

"Give me a ride to the blue house."

She met his eyes and huffed a sigh then nodded as she reached for the car door. Kellie's mustang roared as Mim pressed her foot down on the accelerator.

"You know you should always let your car warm up a few minutes before driving."

Mim revved the car again, and backed quickly out of the driveway.

"You're mad, I can tell."

"I'm not mad, Roger. I just don't understand. You're fooling around in Jacksonville and smoking grass and all you can say is *yeah*."

"I don't want to lie to you. I'm not going to mislead a nice girl like you."

She huffed another breath. "I've been married, Roger. I know what goes on."

"But you're a nice girl, not like … well, look, I know you like me, or at least used to like me. I know about your crummy marriage to what's-his-name. I know you are a kind and sensitive person, too. And I don't want to hurt you. I've been going through …."

Mim's lips pursed as she pulled into the dirt drive way of the blue house. Raising a brow, she shook her head and tittered, "Yeah, I know what you mean. I guess I should be honored."

As he opened the door and leaned back in, Roger rested a hand on the bucket seat. "It's just not the right time. You're lonely, I'm lonely. Lonely people do stupid things."

Mim's eyes widened as she caught her breath.

Don't look so surprised, sister, I know all about you. This is a small town, everybody talks. And you're not the first girl to get into a screwed-up marriage."

"I left."

"You're right, you did. Good for you. But you can't forget about it, can you? You ever get scared when you're thinking about it?" Roger nodded his head. "Yeah, right. You do. You walk around me with kid gloves on, thinking that's what makes you kind and nice, and maybe you should. I've got things going on in my head that you never dreamed about. Bad stuff, Mim. Surfing helps. Too cold to surf now or I'd be out there. And the job helps, but I don't think it's for me.

"You know, you've never asked me anything about me. I just see this, *I feel sorry for the guy from Vietnam* look. You have no idea. We're trying to fight a war with one hand tied behind our back and it's impossible." He was quiet for several moments and began again. "And you, what do you want to do, heal me? Spread your legs and heal me? I can find that anywhere, Mim. And you're too special to let yourself fall into that trap. Keep yourself on that pedestal, Mim and don't let anybody drag you down."

Her heart beating a mile a minute, Mim breathed in and felt the wetness on her cheeks. Roger's words had come so harshly, so cruelly that their meaning had not really soaked in yet. She backed from the parking space, slid into first, then second and motored toward the swing bridge. Her head swirling, she tried to recall the words Roger had said. Was he right?

****

"The world's a mess," Edna Myers muttered. She pulled on the ball of yarn in the basket next to where she was seated and worked the crochet needle through the half-finished scarf she was making. "You young people..." she looked to Mim. "Not you dear, you're fine. It's, well, I just don't understand what all the fuss is about. We are in a war, let these young men fight it! Instead ... well, during World War II it wasn't on the news all the time, and no one would have dreamed of going against our country." She shook her head, pulling once again on the yarn.

"I think some people think we have no business being over there. That this is a political war." Mim lifted a glass of Pepsi Cola to her lips and added, "But I don't understand it either. Kellie writes me now and then, but she never says anything about what is right or wrong. She just talks about how busy she is or how pretty it is over there. You know, the government isn't going to let anyone really write something that could give away the location or what they think might hurt the men."

"Why should they?" Edna retorted. "We need to support those boys, they're dying over there." Her voice rose as she continued, her mouth drawn tightly. Edna yanked hard on the ball of yarn. "And these riots, all this burning down of cities, what in the world is happening? I'm telling you it's just like it says in the Bible. These are the end of days." Edna glanced at her daughter before turning back to the scarf. "You know, I think we ought to ask that nice boy, Roger to come have Thanksgiving dinner with us. What do you think?"

Not knowing what to say, Mim dug into her robe pocket and pulled out Kellie's letter. "Want to read Kellie's letter? She sent a picture too."

Edna leaned forward and grasped it, plucking the photograph from the pages. She studied it for a few moments. "That girl sure has changed. I remember when she was all pimples and so chubby. But Kellie has always been a lovely girl, a very polite young lady."

Edna placed the photo on the side table and opened the pages to read. She giggled at the part where Kellie recounted how the nurses got lost when several of them went to Japan on leave. After that, she quietly read Kellie's concerns for her brother Henry and for Larry.

"That poor girl. She sees the worst of life every day. I imagine she has to be one tough cookie to put up with all that. I hope it doesn't affect her relationships." Edna's eyes searched Mim's. "You know, your uncle Harvey was in World War II." She shook her head. "He never was the same."

For a moment, Mim thought about telling her mother about the encounter with Roger and what they'd talked about, but she thought against it as Edna turned the volume of the news on the television higher.

The newscaster talked about an ongoing battle near Da Nang, and the number of casualties, civilian and military. He talked about Robert McNamara and the escalation of troops and how President Johnson supported his Secretary of State.

A microphone was thrust into one veteran's face as he marched along a road of protesters. "We can't fight this war with one hand tied behind our back," he spouted. Another protester screamed back, "We have no business over there! This is a rich man's war!"

Her eyes widened. Hadn't Roger said *Our hands are tied behind our backs?* Yes, he'd said those very words and then had become suddenly quiet.

CHAPTER 8

Naomi put--or at least tried to put--the LSD episode behind her. Though she felt no different since then, just the memory of it left her feeling used, as if no matter what she did she was damned to having cruel people and cruel things in her life.

"Why doesn't he come home?" she called out as she drove home. The little framed picture of Roy dangling from the rear-view mirror smiled at her, and she wanted to hold that feeling. But she knew that at some point, some newscaster's voice would calmly recount the horror of the war over the radio or on TV, or some protester would shout some hateful words.

"He's doing his job," she called again.

Forcing her thoughts to important, practical things, Naomi loosened her grip on the steering wheel. The car was running fine now; it had been the transmission, like Guy had said. He had let her slide on the payment until Roy's check came in.

They were also letting her slide on the gas, so now she had a full tank--well, nearly. The drive to Miller Motte in Wilmington had taken the gas gauge to just below full. The little Opal station wagon wasn't much to look at with dents in the bumper and front door, but it was great on gas.

Billy, one of the men at Guy's, had said he could pop out the dents and would give the car a paint job for a hundred bucks. Naomi thought about how many days' worth of tips it would take to manage that. "Maybe if I can switch with Janice on the night shift I can swing it," she said aloud as she dug her fingers into the pocket of her waitress uniform. She felt the coins and dollar bills. Dollars were always a treat and Naomi guessed that she probably had around ten dollars including the bills. The men from the dredge working on the ICW had tipped generously. She'd smiled a lot too. *No harm in that*, she thought as her fingers held the coins.

Her eyes scanned the darkening skies as she pulled next to the white fence of her yard. She groaned. "Not again. I'm so tired of rain and I don't care if the farmers need it or not." Looking south toward Topsail Island, the sky was still blue and clear. "Humph, they never get soaked.

Drawing her sweater close around her, Naomi grabbed her hand bag and brown paper bag of seafood and ran inside the two-story house. The kitchen was as she'd left it, clean and smelling of lemons. She loved the fresh aroma and besides, she'd read that putting nine lemons in a bowl would bring wealth, accomplishment, and good luck. She really didn't believe all the nonsense about good luck, but why not give it a try? The Boltons with all their hocus pocus stuff offered a fun distraction and she thought that playing along might be fun and even do a little good.

After setting the bag of seafood in the refrigerator, Naomi walked to the sink to wash her hands and reached for a glass of tap water. From the window she watched the black cat meander around the bushes of the yard. Then suddenly, as if it knew she was thinking of it, the cat turned to her, its one eye catching hers. Its filmy, frosted eye, the one that looked purple, almost matched the pansies and asters she had planted for fall.

"Now that damn cat looks just like my flowers," Naomi exhaled reluctantly. For a moment, she thought of uprooting them and planting something else, something white, or yellow or anything but shades of purple. *Don't sweat the small stuff,* she heard Roy's voice say, and she smiled and reached to flip on the radio. Anticipating swinging sounds from the radio, rather she heard a man's voice. *Three US planes shot down over Hanoi ….* Though the man continued, all Naomi heard was *three US planes*. Her body chilled as she dropped the glass in her hand.

Naomi steadied her body against the counter and, still hearing the words, she felt her knees weaken. She inhaled, closing her eyes, picturing Roy's face, his smiling face and then she saw him dead. "No!" she yelled.

Until you know for sure, don't sweat the small stuff. She opened her eyes. Pitickity wound around one of the posts outside, meowed gently, then louder. Looking at the sky again, hoping to see the constellations, Naomi moaned, wishing the darkness would hurry. "Damn cat, you're bad luck," she growled as she listened to its mewing grow louder.

She stared for a moment at the broken glass on the kitchen floor and thought of gathering the cat, putting it in a box and dropping it off somewhere, anywhere, just somewhere where she could get rid of it. She paused, struggling with the words she'd heard on the radio, knowing in her heart that it had been Roy in one of the planes.

"Maybe I'll drop it at someone's farm or maybe over on the island," Naomi said aloud. She looked at the graying sky again and asked, "What if it rains, would there be time to drop it off before it rains?"

She nodded, thinking how there were always people on the island fishing. "Fish everywhere, there'll always be something for the cat to eat." She rushed to the closet, found the box of old clothes she was accumulating for the church and emptied it, then began calling, "Pitickity, Pitickity, meow, meow, come on little pussycat."

Surprised that the cat responded to her calling so quickly, she bent down as the feline wrapped in between her legs. Gently scooping Pitickity into her arms, Naomi placed the cat in the box, again surprised that it did not put up a fight.

Slowly, she walked back to the kitchen where she'd dropped her keys, all the while talking soothingly to the cat. She carried it outside, and slammed the door behind her.

Shifting the Opal into gear, Naomi made her way south toward Holly Ridge and turned onto Highway 50 toward Topsail Island. Thinking that Mim would know where a good dropping off place would be, she cursed herself for not calling her friend before leaving. The swing bridge was closed to traffic and Naomi watched as a long barge made its way between the pilings. It seemed so close and so large that it would be impossible to fit beneath the bridge, but it did, crooning its long, deep, slow whistle as it passed through.

Stopping at the light in the center of Surf City, she looked right to Mr. Frank's Texaco station. She and Roy usually got inner tubes there in the summer. Ahead was the Superette Shopping Center and Red and White grocery store.

As the light changed, Naomi turned left, accelerating as she passed Batts Cafe. She slipped the stick back into second gear as she eyed the police car parked just to the other side of it.

She heard the low scratching from inside the box and called sweetly to Pitickity, "Don't worry, I've got a nice home for you with someone who will feed you and take care of you." Naomi heard herself lie.

Pitickity scratched more loudly on the box, caterwauled and mewed. One soft black paw reached outside the box as he mewed again softly.

"Poor cat, I can't do this. No." Naomi inhaled and bit her lip.

Black cats are bad luck. Three planes downed. The phrases pulsed and repeated and Naomi slowed the car, looking for a place to turn around, to go back home. She felt herself tremble. Lost in indecision and doubt, she let the tears fall from her eyes. Pulling into a driveway, she paused for a moment, and her eyes fixed on the car parked there. *Isn't this Mim's?* Naomi sat stunned, her chest rising and falling rapidly, her fingers on the wheel, shaking. *Is this where Mim lives?*

Naomi sat mesmerized and shaken, about the cat, about the crazy things the Boltons had said, about the drink at the party and about the three US planes. Was the world crazy or was it just she?

Hands pulling at her hair, she sobbed, and closed her eyes to think of the lemons in the kitchen and of Roy's instructions to not sweat the small stuff, and she laughed, then laughed again as Mim opened the screen door. Poking her head out, she asked, "Is that you, Naomi?"

"Yes," she called as she wiped her face with a tissue.

"I didn't know you knew where I lived. You should have called first."

"No joke, I should have. You are going to think I'm nuttier than a fruitcake when I tell you what I'm doing here."

"Nothing surprises me anymore, Naomi. The world has gone berserk. Momma and I were just watching the news and--"

Naomi shook her head. "I never listen to the news, I don't want to hear a thing," she called from the open car window. "Hop in, I just had to get out of the house. Don't mind the cat."

Opening the screen door, Mim hollered inside, "Momma I'm going scooter-pootin' with Naomi, be back soon."

Mim opened the car door, heard the mewing from the box and, picking it up, settled it in her lap. "So, why do you have a cat in a box?"

"Funniest thing, you're not going to believe it."

"Go on. What's going on? I hope you weren't going to drown this poor thing."

Mim took the lid from the box and reached her hand to pet Pitickity. "Oh, I've seen this cat around. It hangs out around the fishing piers and bait shops. What are you doing with it?"

Naomi eyed the cat, pursing her lips she reached her hand to pet him. "According to my landlord, this is a magic cat, and it's been alive for over fifty years."

"Get outta here. That's ridiculous." Mim scoffed.

"No joke, that's what they said."

"Don't tell me you believe all that, Naomi?"

She shrugged. "Who knows?"

"Poor little kitty," Mim continued stroking the cat as it sat peacefully in the box.

"Yeah," Naomi agreed. "This cat is the cat that caterwauls around my house so loud that it keeps me awake. So, since the neighbors don't want to be responsible for their animals, I will. I thought I'd bring it over here by one of the piers and set it free ... but I've changed my mind."

"This cat looks like the one that hangs out around the piers. There are a lot of wild tom cats around, most are missing an eye or an ear or both. What's its name?"

Naomi shook her head. "Poor Pitickity."

"Poor kitty has been fixed. Did you notice that? Somebody cared enough about this cat to get it fixed." Pushing the box aside, Mim cuddled the cat. "Poor cat, poor Pitickity." She stroked the cat's fur as it leaned against her. "Was this mean old lady going to dump you off?"

"No, I just got upset, I guess. Storm's coming." Naomi checked the skies. "Sometimes everything gets to me, Mim. I think I'm going nuts."

"Want to go for a ride and talk about it?"

Naomi backed from Mim's driveway.

"Go north, toward the blue house."

Naomi drove slowly the mile or so and turned off the ignition. Reaching for Pitickity, she cuddled him in her lap. "Sorry old boy."

"Somebody told me that we all do crazy things when we're lonely. You're lonely Naomi, you miss Roy and you're worried. I hear about what's going on. I'm not blind or stupid."

"I never thought you were, Mim. To tell the truth, I never really thought much about things like that before, not before Roy enlisted. And now …." Parked in the dirt driveway of the blue house, Naomi stared at the figure of a man walking their way. He came from behind the stack of concrete blocks.

Roger smoothed his blonde hair, loose and caught in the breeze, to behind his ears. "What are you two doing out here?"

"Just shooting the breeze," Mim tittered.

"Good night for it." He leaned against Mim's window. "Taking the cat along for a ride?"

"Long story," Naomi said.

"Is this your cat?"

"It must be, I guess." She folded the cat close to her and stroked his fur.

"Strange. All I have to say about people from the Sneaky Freaky, they are sneaky and freaky."

Naomi laughed. "Look at the pot calling the kettle black." Opening the door, Naomi walked toward the dunes, leaving Mim and Roger alone.

"Now, I've heard of taking your dog for a walk on the beach, but a cat?"

"It's complicated."

"Life always is, Mim. But I have a feeling that Naomi has a tough row to hoe. I know about Roy. It's starting to wear on her."

Mim was quiet for a few moments, wondering what Roger was doing at the blue house. She began, "Why--"

"Nice seeing you. Oh, here? I come here a lot. You should know that. Great place for thinking."

"Yeah."

"What were you going to do with the cat anyway?"

"I think she was going to drop it off somewhere, but had a change of heart." Mim watched Naomi still walking toward the dunes. "It's not hers, not really."

"Looks like it is now. Sometimes a change of heart is good." Roger stumbled the words, gulping as he pulled a hand through his hair again.

Her eyes met his and held, she knew he was not talking about the cat and Naomi.

He turned to go.

"Wait, are you still detecting, uh, I mean a detective?"

Roger smiled. "Yeah, helping Jason in the Ferry. Seems somebody, some transient up from Florida is bringing in pot."

Mim cocked her head, and raised a brow. "Should you be doing this? I mean, isn't that something you may ...."

Laughing, his head thrown back, Roger said, "This guy is a dealer. Sells tons of the stuff."

"Still ...."

He turned to go again. "I'll buy you a cheeseburger at the Sand Piper if you want to meet me on Saturday."

"Okay."

"Around four."

"Okay."

Mim called to Naomi, who was now standing near a small dune just north of the blue house. Turning, she made her way back across the vacant lot of sand spurs and wild grasses. She nodded to Roger as she neared.

"Things have been very strange the last few days, Roger. Don't mind me or Pitickity."

"Roy?"

Naomi nodded.

"I heard something on the news about planes being shot down and I worried for you. I know your husband is a pilot."

"A bombardier."

"Oh."

Nodding again, Naomi stroked the cat, her fingers reaching into its fur, feeling bumps and lines of scarring. "I have lemons on my counter for good luck."

Mim nodded and Roger smiled and said nothing as Naomi moved into the driver's seat of her car. Mim shrugged as she slid into the passenger side. "Guess we're going now, nice seeing you."

Roger grinned and waved as the women pulled away.

"I have this little pendant." Naomi reached into her blouse and pulled out the copper and purple token Norwood had given her. "And I don't walk under ladders or do anything with the number thirteen. I'm trying to be so careful."

Mim's hand rested on her friend's shoulder. "I do pray for you every night Naomi, for your husband. Really, I do."

"Thank you." She paused, feeling the nails of Pitickity knead her thighs. "That's probably a lot better than all the other stuff, but when I heard the news, and the party the other night, well ...." she tittered. "It was a real trip."

"What party? Trip? What are you talking about?"

"It was Halloween night. I went with Vickie, we went out behind the race track in Holly Ridge to some old house. Some kids I went to school with were there."

"I know Vickie," Mim said. "Well, not real well, but I know who you're talking about."

"Someone put something in my drink and it made me feel funny, like or I guess, like drugs."

Aghast at the words, Mim instantly thought of that night and Roger and how he acted."

"Was it marijuana?"

"No, I didn't smoke anything, Mim. Don't you know anything?"

"It's all drugs …."

"Well, it wasn't pot. Someone, I think it was Elmo, put LSD or something like it in my drink. Vickie said I did things … I don't even remember most of it.

"Elmo," Mim pondered the name. "Your grade?"

"Yeah, he was in my class, black hair, wore it in a buzz cut back then. Well now, it's down past his ears.

"Oh yeah, he was a goofy kind of kid. He'd come up behind me and say something about racing or something like that, never made any sense."

"That's him, still goofy. He went to get me a drink and after that everything went so strange."

Naomi drove slowly, toward the north end of the island. Passing the Scotch Bonnet Pier and Ocean City she relaxed and propped her left leg on the seat of the car, steering with her right hand as she began opening up to Mim about Halloween night, about Roy, the Boltons, and all of her fears.

CHAPTER 9

"I guess I'll take him back home with me. No sense in fiddlefarting around here." Naomi smiled as she pulled into Mim's driveway. Lifting her eyes skyward she sighed. "Looks like y'all missed the storm again." She nodded north toward Sneads Ferry.

"Daddy used to say that the ocean breezes keep lots of storms away."

"Your daddy was right. It's pouring over at my place."

Mim tittered as she placed Pitickity back in the box, "Bye-bye little kitty cat." Walking around to the driver's side window, she reached in and hugged Naomi. "I'm always here to talk if you like. I'm a phone call away. And Roger was right when he told you not to worry about things until you know for sure."

Naomi nodded. "It's all at once, the Boltons and their--"

"Oh, I wouldn't worry about them. You know, everybody has something weird about them. It's kind of an honor that they would tell you so much."

"Then Elmo …."

"He always was a creep."

"And the planes." Naomi lifted her eyes to Mim. "If you hear anything about where the planes went down will you call and tell me?"

Mim nodded, and stepping back from the car, watched Naomi back from the driveway.

****

In class, the pop quiz was easy, and Mim knew she aced it. Naomi had helped her study. She leaned forward to glimpse her new friend, and both gave the thumbs up sign. Of course it was a breeze for Naomi, she'd always been smart. But for Mim things were a little more difficult, especially shorthand. The characters didn't seem to stick in her memory as they should. And as for etiquette class, all the walking perfectly and weighing the right amount seemed ridiculous, especially with the popular trends leaning to having a free spirit. She knew plenty of people who didn't hold themselves just so, that were just as fine as they could be. Her friend Kellie came to mind, with her tousled hair and chubby thighs. But then, the Navy had squared her away. As Kellie had explained, "There's no time to be untidy."

It seemed Naomi didn't have to try at all. Whether it was white gloves and a perfect up-do, or jeans and pigtails, Naomi fit right into one as easily as the other. Whatever it was, Naomi seemed to give off the right vibe effortlessly.

"Hey," Naomi bumped into Mim gently. "I want to go to Cherry Point this Saturday night. Come with me."

"Where's Cherry Point?"

"The other side of Jacksonville, around New Bern."

"Why?"

"I got a call from Roy. He took R and R in Hong Kong and made a call." Her face beamed and she threw back her head. "He's fine, and knew I would be worrying about him. He wants me to go out and have fun, *but not too much.*" She winked.

"Really?"

Rocking back on her heels against the wall, Naomi closed her eyes. "I want to dance. I'm not going to do anything wrong, miss fuddy-duddy, just dance."

"I'm not--"

"Don't you want to do something besides wait tables and study? You haven't gone out with anyone since you got back from Detroit, have you? That's what you said the other day and this guy Roger--"

Naomi flipped her hand in the air. "He's nice enough, but has he asked you out?

"We're friends."

"I didn't ask you if you were friends, I asked if he had asked you out on a date."

"No, he hasn't. It's best if we stay friends."

"Then, forget about him or at least don't sit around pining for him." Naomi rolled her eyes. "I mean, what a bummer. That must have made you feel like whale shit when *you* asked him to ask you out."

Mim couldn't remember the last time she'd been on a date.

"Little Miss Mim, you need to do something besides mourn your misbegotten marriage and stop fawning over some guy who won't make a move."

For a moment Mim regretted having bared her soul the day she and Naomi had driven the island. Still, she knew Naomi was right.

"Well …."

"Life is passing you by, Mim. I'm either going with or without you, so what do you say?"

****

Mim parked her car by the street next to Dixon High School and waited for Naomi to pull in behind her. They'd be driving Naomi's Opal Cadet to Cherry Point. But before they got underway, Naomi stepped out from the car, her hands on her hips, her hair teased high. She twirled a couple of times and said, "What do you think? Too short?"

"I wouldn't bend over if I were you."

The burgundy mini-skirt came just a tad higher than mid-thigh. The matching vest, accentuating her slim waist, reached to nearly the same length. Naomi's fingers fluffed the ruffled collar and billowy sleeves of the white blouse, and then she stomped her white go-go boots on the pavement.

"I'm hip, about as hip as you can be."

"I'll have to admit that. You sure are. You certainly didn't skimp on the eye-liner and eye shadow either. When I was living in Detroit, I used to wear lots of make-up when I went out."

"Why did you quit?"

Mim shrugged. "I don't know, I kind of like the natural look and besides, I'm a beach girl."

Naomi crossed her legs at the ankles, crossed her arms and eyed Mim's outfit: a mid-thigh paisley dress with brown sandals. "Hair could be better, but we'll fix that at the dance. And honey," she fingered the brass pendant around her neck, "I know you know how to dress for dancing." She shook her head. "And you have a great figure. At least you have boobs, I have none at all." Laughing, Naomi crossed her arms across her chest. "Hmm, I was thinking about how you and I are really not that different. We both got married right out of high school. But I had a wonderful husband, I still do. You had a nightmare. And to tell the truth, you need to get out and have fun a lot more than I do." She tapped her foot, deciding if Mim's outfit was hip enough. "You'll do, let's go."

Mim and Naomi walked into the Brass Dolphin, then walked directly to the bathroom. Already there was a line of girls waiting for an empty stall. Naomi leaned into the mirror and preened her hair and long, dangly earrings. Opening her makeup bag, she handed Mim the eye-liner, and watched as Mim streamlined her eyes. Teasing her hair a bit higher and replacing the headband, Mim pulled small tendrils from the side and held out an open hand. "Hairspray," she said, as if a doctor asking for a scalpel.

She borrowed Naomi's lipstick and eyeshadow, too, and folded the waist of her skirt to shorten it. "Ready?" she asked.

"Groovy."

CHAPTER 10

"That short one with the black hair sure could dance. You danced with him too, didn't you?" Naomi unlocked the car door and slid inside.

Mim nodded. "Out of all the guys he was the best dancer."

"Did he ask you out?"

"No, he just said he'd be back next Saturday and asked if I was coming back."

"Wasn't his name Chuck or Buck or something like that?" Slipping into third gear, Naomi turned onto Highway 17 toward Dixon School, where Mim's car was parked.

Mim answered, "Bucky. He sure was a cutie."

"That's what you need, Mim, somebody to just have fun with. Don't get into any serious stuff. What about that tall one from New York? I couldn't understand a word he said."

"When he slow danced with me, he kept trying to stick his tongue in my ear." Mim grimaced.

"Yuck. Me too. He told me he was being shipped out to Vietnam and wanted something to remember me by."

Mim laughed, "Yeah, I bet I know what that was, but how about the guy from Texas? Now he was a terrible dancer, but I felt sorry for him."

Naomi shook her head. "Just one dance was enough for me, two left feet. But I sure did like his buddy, he's a pilot too. We talked, said he was familiar with the *Constellation*, Roy's ship. He reminded me of Roy too." Glimpsing her watch, she yawned. "This is the first time I've been out this late in a long time."

"Me too," echoed Mim. "It's nearly one-thirty, I hope my mother isn't waiting up." She leaned back against the seat; Naomi had found a slow blues station, so Mim listened to the Righteous Brothers sing "Unchained Melody". A few more songs played or she must have drifted off, because before Mim knew it, Naomi was jostling her awake and shooing her into her own car.

"Be careful driving. The cops are out on Saturday nights and those in Holly Ridge will get you in a second."

"This was a good idea, thanks for suggesting it and you're right, I need to move on and quit thinking of what *might* happen."

* * * *

Naomi pulled the car next to the white picket fence and, stopping to lean against the little maple tree in the yard, looked up at the sky. She could make out the Big Dipper and the Little Dipper just fine and then her eyes searched for Cassiopeia. "The big W," she giggled, thinking of the movie *It's a Mad, Mad, Mad, Mad World* and the reference to the big W in that film. The place where the riches were hidden. She and Roy had seen the movie together at the Bijou in Wilmington and when he'd found Cassiopeia it just seemed fitting. The big W would always be their reference to happiness and every time they looked in the sky to see it, the constellation would reaffirm their happiness and love.

Leaning her head back, Naomi studied the stars. She concentrated on them and, touching the pendant around her neck, prayed. Whispering her love, her longing and faith in his safety, she imagined Roy's smell and her face buried in the warmth of his neck.

She thought of the last time he had been home on leave and how they'd motored to Lea Island and to Topsail. She thought of their love making, the small birthmark on his right hip, shaped like an anchor. That had meaning too. Everything had meaning. The Boltons, the strange Boltons … Naomi wondered why Roy had never explained them to her.

Of course, she thought, it must have been so that she could find them in her own time and way.

Pitickity had meaning. Hadn't she nearly thrown him away? But she hadn't. He needed love too, even if he was ugly. Naomi chuckled at the thought.

And then there was the drink, Elmo, the acid trip. And though it had been terrifying, she had come through. Closing her eyes, she recalled the clouds and the words they had formed: peace, love, sex. All beautiful things, and the way it had made her feel, the way it had made her feel like Roy was right there. She had felt him that night, really felt him.

All of these things, the Boltons, the cat, the constellations and the trip, they had to be signs and omens from Roy too.

What had followed, the fear, the screaming, she didn't really remember those things. She felt her heart beat quicken as she struggled to recall what exactly had happened, but past the clouds, there was nothing.

Naomi opened her eyes to the sky again and the big W. She breathed in the cool, salty air. Even from where she stood, she could hear the ocean in the distance. It was so still, with the stars, so quiet with her love in the sky. Most certainly, Roy was looking at the constellations right now. Naomi knew it.

CHAPTER 11

Thanksgiving

Roger pushed the shopping cart through the lane lined with cans of vegetables. He slowly passed the canned potatoes, the lima beans and baked beans. *What was it she wanted?* he asked himself. *Corn and green beans … and onions.* His eyes scanned the shelves and caught the beans and then the corn. A bit farther down the aisle he spied a small jar of pearl onions.

Moving on as his eyes scanned the shelves, Roger nearly bumped into another shopper. "Excuse me." He shook his head and pulled the cart back.

The Red and White grocery store bustled; it was one of the few times of the year that it did, during off-tourist season. Making his way towards a checkout lane, Roger lined up behind an older man, his hands full of fresh green collards. The man turned and grinned. "Collard greens, it's not Thanksgiving without them."

Roger nodded and grinned.

The man continued, "You're not from here, are you?"

"No, how could you tell?"

"Canned vegetables. Only city folk eat that stuff."

"Oh," Roger guffawed. He thought for a moment, trying to recall if Mim had specified which, fresh or canned vegetables. "Excuse me," Roger spoke the words apologetically as he moved out of line and rolled the cart down the canned vegetable aisle then hurried to the produce section of the store to grab the items Mim had requested.

It was only 11 a.m. and dinner was to be served at 3 p.m. He hoped he wasn't too late and then he thought of the collards the man at the store had. Were Mim and her mother preparing collards? "It's so southern." He grimaced.

This was something new for him, having dinner with someone other than his own family. But then, that had always been a trying experience, all the arguing that eventually turned into yelling. And last year, his first Thanksgiving back from Vietnam, he'd spent it with Jason and his family. That had been pleasant, but they had no children, so it had just been the three of them, and they had eaten in silence.

Yes, he was grateful, but nervous, afraid he'd say the wrong thing. Or hear something that would trigger a bad memory, a memory of something unforgiving, unpredictable. Roger never knew what the outcome would be or how he would react, or if the image of Barnes, sitting next to him, and his brains bursting from his head, would ever leave him.

That was the most scary, perhaps: not knowing if he could handle it, or at least act normal. But then, normal had been changing a lot since Nam. Normal now came in different forms. Surfing was a form, sex was a form; they had been the only ways that helped the images fade.

Roger pulled money from his wallet and paid the cashier, the color red still in his head. He smiled at the cashier, the sounds still in his head. He nodded-- the sights and sounds still in his head. He could almost smell it now as he walked to his car. Opening the door, he set the groceries on the passenger seat.

In his mind, the kid was dancing, the kid was Barnes or Barnes was the kid. The kid turned and swirled, his arms held out as he moved closer to the men.

Dancing and laughing, the kid stepped again and then he reached inside his shirt and pulled ... on something. He'd been close enough, and that day they'd lost four guys.

Nobody wanted to hear those stories. Certainly, Mim would never understand them. They would frighten her, especially if she knew that he had pulled the trigger on a woman. It didn't matter that she'd had a gun, too. The rule was, you don't kill women and children, or that was the way it was supposed to be.

"But what about when …." Roger spoke aloud and, hearing his own voice, felt the pull of wanting normalcy and how much he was looking forward to Thanksgiving with Mim and her family.

He thought of how nice it was for her to invite him to Thanksgiving Dinner. Despite the arguments and misunderstanding between them, he liked Mim. She was genuine, and had been through some tough times. Roger chuckled. "Certainly, none of the women I've been with in Jacksonville are going to make me a Thanksgiving dinner."

After driving slowly north to the blue house, Roger stepped from his car and pulled a tightly rolled joint from his jeans pocket. He lit it and pulled a few deep drags and held them. He felt the smoke creep into his head, relaxing him as he leaned against the car. His ears caught the thunder of waves crashing to shore just behind him and beyond the dunes. His nostrils filled with the soft scent of salt air.

"Nice," he whispered.

* * * *

"These are the best darn collards I've ever eaten." Amos Burger licked his bottom lip, and caught Edna Myers' eye. "You are one good cook, my lady."

"Thank you, Amos. I'm glad you and Gloria could join us for Thanksgiving." She nodded to their son Alex, who was eating quietly. "Maybe after dinner, honey, you can go play on the beach, I know there'll be some other kids out there running around on the dunes.

Alex lifted his head and smiled. "Yes ma'am, that sounds fine."

"You have a very well-behaved son, Gloria."

"Thank you, Edna. Sometimes he can be a handful though." Gloria smiled and added, "I've never been able to cook collards. It's a southern dish and I guess no matter how long I'm down here in the south, I'll always be a northerner."

Edna tittered, "Now you and Amos have been down here long enough that you're honorary southerners and I can give you the secret to making greens if you like. It's not that difficult."

Slicing several slices of turkey, Amos asked, "Anyone? I'm carving, just need to know how many slices."

"I'll have another." Roger held his plate toward the head of the table where Amos sat. "And some of that sweet potato casserole."

Mim scooped a large serving spoon full onto Roger's plate, careful to get plenty of crispy brown marshmallows on top.

"Thanks for getting the beans and corn, Roger. I completely forgot the other day when I went shopping"

"My pleasure Mim. I'm very thankful that you guys asked me over for Thanksgiving. I can't remember how long it's been since I had such a good meal. I even liked the collards."

"Two, you had *two* helping of collards, now I'd say you liked them." Edna grinned.

"Yes ma'am. They were delicious."

Alex looked to his mother and asked, "May I be excused?"

"No dessert?" Asked Edna.

"No ma'am, I'm full." Turning to his mother, he asked for permission once again.

"Okay, but if there's no one else out there, come back."

Alex leaned in to kiss his mother and father, then scampered out the front door.

"I'm glad I didn't make him get all dressed up for dinner, Edna. I hope you don't mind. But I knew he'd want to go play with the other kids who have finished their dinners too."

"Don't you worry one bit about that, they need to get out and play." Edna shook her head. "So many children are sitting in front of the television, just glued to it. They need to be outdoors playing."

Gloria nodded.

Amos leaned back in his chair, pushing his plate a few inches away. "Pumpkin pie?"

Mim rose, "I'll be right back. Coffee anyone?"

Returning in a few moments, Mim carried a tray full of cups and saucers and slices of pie. Settling pie and coffee in front of everyone, she boasted, "I made the pie."

"Yes, Mim gave me a rest this year and she made the whole dinner."

"Except the collards," Mim chimed.

"Including the dessert. I do believe she has a pecan pie back in the kitchen too."

Amos lifted his chin. "Um, I love pecan pie."

Mim rose again, walked to the kitchen, and returned with two pecan pies. "Here you are." Settling herself in a chair, Mim turned to Roger. His eyes already on her, he winked.

What does that mean? Mim wondered, and she cocked her head.

"I think he's flirting with you," guffawed Amos. Sipping the remainder of his coffee, he held out his cup.

"Amos?" his wife scolded. They're not here to serve you."

Edna rose. "That's alright, I should have brought the coffee pot out here, anyways."

Amos patted his belly and sipped from the fresh cup Edna had poured. He pushed a little farther from the table and turned his attention to Roger. "So, you were in Vietnam." Without waiting for an answer, he continued. "I was in the big one, World War II. Now *that* was hell. I never saw so many dead bodies. We were in Italy. Those Italians," Amos shook his head and laughed. "Dumb as doorknobs, but the women. Now the women are beautiful."

Gloria Burger rolled her eyes.

"How many of those gooks do you think you killed?" Amos asked.

His jaw having tightened, Roger tried to relax. "A few, I guess."

"I hear it's pretty bad, lots of jungle. Now we didn't have any jungle to hide in, we had everything right out in the open."

Roger's jaw clamped tighter and, turning his head away, his eyes met Mim's.

They were asking, but she didn't understand, not until she heard Amos ask another question.

"I keep hearing that you guys are baby killers. I know that has to be a lie. But then you can't help it if a bomb's dropped and civilians get it, now, can you?"

Reaching her leg forward, Mim searched for Roger's and found it. She lay it next to his and met his eyes again, pressing her foot as close as she could to his.

"This is a different war, Mr. Burger."

"Damn right it's a different war. We had all kind of support from the government and we were doing without meat and doing without tires and rubber and all kinds of things to help our men over there. This damn president doesn't know his ass from his elbow."

Roger chuckled. "Well, we agree there."

"Enough talk about war, Amos," Gloria interjected, "Enough politics, you should know better than that, being on the town council. You know you have to be careful about what you say, though I know we are among friends that may feel the same."

Amos nodded and reached for another slice of pie.

Edna, Mim and Gloria began gathering the leftover bowls of food and walked toward the kitchen.

"Sorry about my husband. Sometimes he goes on and on. He's got his opinions, and I know he saw some action in Europe, but mostly his unit was there for clean-ups. Looking at his service records, I don't think he was ever in any big campaigns. He tries to act like he was a big shot during the war, but he wasn't. Don't let him fool you."

Turning to Mim, Gloria touched her shoulder. "I'm sorry for your boyfriend, Mim. I know he must have had it bad. It's in his eyes. And I've come to find out that if they brag about it, it usually isn't true. Roger is pretty closed mouth about the whole thing."

"He's just a friend, not a boyfriend." Mim scooped the remaining sweet potato casserole into a smaller dish and set it in the refrigerator. "But he is a nice guy and you're right, he does not talk about it."

CHAPTER 12

Hey buddy,

Just thought I'd drop you a line and see how you're doing. Thought it was a coincidence that I'm living where that nurse you liked in Nam lived. I know she's still on the Repose.

I met a chick that is good friends with her. Seems they grew up together on this little barrier island, Topsail, just south of Camp Lejeune, and they write pretty regular. Her name is Mim and I had Thanksgiving dinner with her family. Hope yours was as good as mine.

She'll mention Kellie every once in a while, and so it sounds like Kellie still thinks about you, though I don't think she's pining too much, if you know what I mean.

She doesn't know that I know you or if she does, she hasn't mentioned it. I don't talk about it. Been doing a lot of surfing when it's warm here. The

*water here in North Carolina doesn't really start
warming up until around April so I've got a few
months before I can get back to it. It helps a lot to
get my mind off of things. You know what I mean.*

*I guess I told you about this detective I've been
working with. We're working on a case in Sneads
Ferry. Seems somebody has been bringing in kilos of
pot. Nice job, huh? Hope I find out before he does.
Ha ha.*

*Write me and let me know how it's hanging. You
know man, Kellie isn't going to mind if you only got
half a leg, you got the most import one between
your legs, right? Ha ha. I still think you ought to let
me give her your address.*

*Hang loose,
Roger*

*P.S. You ought to come out here for a visit
sometime, it's real peaceful. People are nice too.*

Larry folded the letter into its envelope and set it
on the table next to him. He leaned back and
thought about Roger. They'd been buddies in Nam.

You're one lucky bastard. Those had been the last
words Larry had spoken to him before he'd shipped
out. *You're getting outta here.*

It wasn't true that the North Vietnamese were as
good as soldiers as the U.S. They couldn't match

them in firepower or skill as fighting men, but they came up with ways to hurt the morale of the men and to disable them. They used all kinds of booby traps to injure them so they couldn't return to battle.

One such trap was punji sticks, sharpened bamboo stakes, smeared with shit and any other bodily fluid that would cause severe infection. They'd take the sticks and put them in a hole, points upward, and cover them with a thin frame so that when the victim stepped there the spikes entered his body through the foot.

Smacking his stump aside his leg, he chuckled. "We're not in Kansas anymore, are we, Roger?"

Leaning back in the recliner, Larry clicked the remote-control volume up. Two actors dressed as cowboys stood in the center of a dusty small-town street. The camera zoomed in on the fingers of one of the cowboys nervously twitching against the handle of his holstered gun.

The camera then zoomed in on the face of the opposing man, dressed in buckskin chaps, his holster slung low on his hips. His eyes narrowing, he called out to the nervous man. *I don't wanna kill you Buck, but them cattle ain't yours. We kill cattle rustlers out here.*

Resting the remote on the arm of the recliner, Larry pulled the wooden arm on the side of the chair and slid back into a reclining position.

Certainly, the star of the show was not going to get killed, but still, it was intriguing as to just how shot up one or each of the cowboys would get. Larry called out, "Hey Mom, can you make some popcorn and bring me a glass of water?"

"Get it yourself," the voice from the kitchen called back. "And turn that darn shoot-em-up down."

Larry turned the volume down slightly, raised his voice above that and called out again, "Get it for me, Mom. I can't do it. You know I can't do it."

"Yes, you can."

He heard the kitchen door slam. His eyes focused on the two gunfighters and as the music intensified, he quickly turned the channel. Waiting a few seconds, he flipped back to the channel and picked the story up. The nervous guy had been wounded and the other man was now apologizing to him, explaining that he had to do it.

"Humph." Larry flipped to *Laugh-In*. Goldie Hawn was dancing in a bikini. Words were painted on her body and she was smiling her *deer in the headlight* look.

"Larry, you have a cane, crutches and a prosthesis. Use them."

He'd not heard his mother re-enter the kitchen, if she'd ever left at all. His eyes looked into hers as she entered the room, first scowling, then sympathetic. He preferred the scowling.

"Your father would have never put up with this," Doris Bodell scolded. "He'd have torn your ass up for sitting around here feeling all sorry for yourself."

"He had both legs."

"He was in World War II." Doris turned and walked back to the kitchen.

Larry turned the volume to the television louder. "I'm not Dad," he yelled after her.

Doris sat at the kitchen table and turned the volume to her own television set louder. Her lips pursed, angry that her son sat so depressed, so determined to let misery ruin his life. She leaned to turn the channel and caught Shirley Booth in a maid's uniform with her hands on her hips. She laughed as Hazel, the maid, ran after Mr. Baxter. She could hear the loud noises from the living room and wondered why her son always watched such violence on television. Hadn't he seen enough of that in Vietnam? She wondered why the veteran's administration had not returned her calls. Wasn't he supposed to go to the hospital for some kind of rehabilitation? It seemed as if no one cared at all for the young men fighting for their country.

There were so many questions, each one filling her with ambivalent feelings about her son, the war, and as of late the country in which she lived. Hadn't it been only a couple of weeks since she'd heard on the news how the Secretary of Defense, Robert McNamara had been mobbed when he was speaking at Harvard University? What was going on in the world? It made no sense. Doris was proud of her son; he had given part of himself for his country, yet all the news was about how horrible the war was.

But war is horrible, she thought. Her own brother had been killed in the Pacific, during World War II, his boat sunk by a German U-boat. His body had never been found.

Once again, Larry called from the living room. "Hey Mom, you gotta see this."

His voice sounded cheerful, and Doris rushed to stand next to his recliner.

"This commercial, have you seen it?"

Turning toward the set, his mother stood, hands on hips, watching as a man stood in front of an automobile. The hood was open and steam rose from the radiator. A woman, his mother-in-law, sneered angrily at him, her eyes giving the *I told you so* look. Then he poured Dow anti-freeze into the radiator, and suddenly, all is well. The next shot showed the mother-in-law with her with bags in hand, entering a taxi while the man waved to her from the front porch.

Doris Bodell tittered loudly, "Yes, that is funny." And then she said it, words she wished she could have put back in her mouth: "I guess I'll never be a mother-in-law, so I'll never have to worry about that." She clasped her hand over her mouth. "Oh,

Larry I'm so sorry. The commercial is funny and I'm sure that one day--"

"Don't kid yourself, Mom. Nobody is going to want me like this." He pulled a pack of cigarettes from his shirt pocket and lit one.

"I wish you wouldn't smoke, dear."

"Why, is it bad for my health?"

She thought of how he'd been when he'd first came home from Vietnam and how he'd struggled. How often had she lay in her bed listening to his labored breathing? It had taken weeks before he'd recovered from that. They were now calling that condition ARDS; the last doctor they'd been to had mentioned how fortunate her son was, as some had died from the disease. "Remember," she said, "the doctor--"

"Oh yeah, DaNang lung," he laughed, "I beat that, didn't I?" He laughed again.

"You see, darling, if you can beat that--"

"I don't want to hear it. You've seen what's going on, the nightly news. Lyndon Baines Johnson, *the President*, they're out to kill us all one way or another. They don't give a damn."

"Oh dear, I wish you wouldn't use that language."

He rolled his eyes. "Son of a bitch Johnson, how about that, Mom? Does that sound better? 'Cause he is one. You know, Mom, I could tell you stories ...."

She knew stories, she'd heard them from her friends, from the mothers of sons who had come back different. A few like her son, physically changed, others angry and drug addicted. Nancy Lowe's son, barely even able to write his own name, he'd been drafted. How could a government do that?

She felt worse for those whose sons had come home in a box. And it was like Larry proclaimed, as if their child's life had meant nothing. No one gave a damn. It was as if the country was glad they were dead because they had been in Vietnam. Just that morning at the hair salon, one of the stylists had commented, *Well, he shouldn't have gone if he didn't want to die.*

What were these boys supposed to do, flee to Canada, live in shame? Doris thought of the signs and slogans and of how ignorant they all sounded, how foolish the young people sounded and looked with their protest signs and peace signs. Did they not understand what communism was? Did they not care about their country? They all seemed so selfish, so bent on fulfilling superficial desires. And then it seemed too, that there were those in the government who agreed with them. "I hate them all! I hate them all!" she yelled.

His eyes flying to hers, Larry reached for his mother's hand. Noticing her trembling lips, he leaned forward. "I'll get the popcorn Mom."

CHAPTER 13

Kellie leaned against the railing of the USS *Repose* and flicked her last cigarette into the ocean. She'd been trying to quit, though had put little effort into doing so. She watched a Huey as it moved away from the ship. It was taking a few of the injured to Japan. They would get more help there and more than likely move on back to the states after that.

It had been a good couple of days. Only a couple of men had arrived, and they did not have anything life-threatening. One had stepped in a punji stick trap, and the weapon had pierced the Marine's boot and little toe. Even that required immediate attention against severe infection, but this time it didn't require an amputation.

Damn Punji sticks. Kellie had seen countless injuries from the damn traps. She'd seen injuries like the latest minor one to life-destroying injuries. There was one where a Marine stepped through a booby trap and the punji stick had risen clear from his leg into his groin. She'd seen them go as far as into the bowel area. Kellie hated the Viet Cong for their torture techniques.

A punji stick injury had been Larry's ticket home. She thought of him often. Not as often as she once had, since there hadn't been a word, not even a letter since he'd left for the states. How was he adjusting? Had he begun using a prosthesis? Was his head right, or was he like so many, damaged and alone? Larry had been lucky compared to some. Or, was it that he preferred a cool beer to the drugs? Kellie hoped that was still the case.

Her thoughts drifted to the sights and sounds in the distance. Ashore, the skies were clear, and if there was any fighting going on, there was no sign.

Why didn't he ever write?

Corpsman Burke moved next to her, rubbing his shoulder against hers. "Margie says she won't be back in the room for at least an hour. I'm stuck aboard for a while."

Taking his fingertips in her own, Kellie cooed, "Come on big boy, I think you need some R and R."

****

Corpsman Burke was married. But Kellie and he had that understanding, the one where there were no strings. Kellie was glad there weren't any. He certainly was not the type of guy she would want to be serious about. For one, his feet always smelled and she'd come to asking him to leave his shoes on when they made trips to her room.

He was kind and polite, did not assume too many things, and spent time to make her feel special. Kellie supposed that he pretended she was his wife or at least someone he truly cared about. They were friends.

He filled a need, and after Larry's departure and going through the *I'll show him that somebody wants me* phase, Kellie realized it would be very easy to get a reputation. It was better to stick with one man. Besides, she could never be serious about being with someone who cheated on his wife. A double standard, she'd been told, but a sin she was willing to live with, since after all, it was war.

As soon as she or he were sent back to the states, the relationship would be over, that was understood, and so Kellie never asked about the wife he never mentioned and neither of them exchanged stateside addresses. She assumed he was from somewhere in the Midwest, since he lacked any type of accent.

Waving good-bye as Corpsman Burke boarded the Huey, Kellie plucked a cigarette from the pack of a nurse beside her.

"Hey, I thought you were quitting?" the nurse asked.

"I've given myself until after the new year."

"1967, hope it's a better year."

Kellie was quiet as she inhaled from the Salem.

"Are you signing back up?"

Kellie nodded.

"Me too."

The women looked toward the land almost twelve miles away. Mountains stood silhouetted in the distance. A curtain of dusky darkness pressed against the sky, and the women saw the silent bursts of brightness. Kellie inhaled again. "Won't be long now," she offered, matter-of-factly.

"Nope." The nurse pulled a cigarette from the pack and brought the lighter to its tip. Cupping her hands against the rising breeze, she inhaled to light it. "Damn, I wish that was fox fire." Exhaling the smoke, she added, "Hope it ain't anybody I know."

CHAPTER 14

Thanksgiving dinner had been great, even the collards. It had been nice feeling normal around ordinary people again. Mim had been nice, not at all as judgmental as she had appeared Halloween night. Grinning broadly, Roger brought the marijuana cigarette to his lips and inhaled, thinking of how delicious the dinner had been.

"I've decided I like collards," he called out. *I wish everyday was like that,* except for the old dude, the Amos fellow. He was in *the big war.* "What a wind bag." Roger tittered, "but his wife put him in his place pretty quick."

Roger didn't want to think about war or windbags. All he wanted was to be that normal guy, the one who'd been at Mim's house, who didn't feel threatened or judged. He wanted to fit in, to be like every other normal person.

****

It was a dark and stormy night, the wind howled through the trees, beating the leafless limbs of the tree against her window... Naomi read the first few words of the novel again. She rolled her eyes and heard the rumble of thunder outside her own window. "Another dark and stormy night," she growled.

Her eyes returned to the page and she searched for the last sentence she'd read.

Lucy heard the soft footsteps on the stairs, the creak from the one step and she pulled the covers up to her neck. It was the third step from the top that always creaked. She bit her bottom lip and thought of the gun in the drawer in the cabinet across the room.

Yes, they were familiar words, though still not sounding any better than the first time she'd tried to read the book. Naomi thumbed to the stamped date at the back of the book. "Poop, I'm late. I need to take it back to the library."

Thinking of how she hated to waste a book, she let her eyes read further.

Horace leaned against the hall wall, holding his breath, a bouquet of flowers in one hand, he hoped he would not be caught by the lovely Lucy before opening the door to her room and pronouncing his deep love for her. She was the love of his life. Though they had never been formally introduced, his love pounded in his chest as he dreamed of holding her against his breast.

"Oh yuck, this is so ..." Naomi growled, "this is ridiculous, who does that? If a guy snuck up on me like that, I *would* grab the gun from the drawer." Closing the worn paperback novel, Naomi sighed and reached for the remote. The color television burst alive with Johnny Carson delivering his nightly monologue on *The Tonight Show*. *He's handsome*, she thought, and, listening to his jokes and references to famous movie stars, Naomi relaxed against the headboard of her bed. Soon, Ed McMahon introduced Carnac the Magnificent.

Naomi loved Carnac, and she watched as Carson, dressed as an all-knowing seer, answered the questions to letters sent in by make-believe fans. Naomi laughed as one joke after another came. Then came the interruption. The room went dark as lightning popped in the air. She held her breath, her mind blank for only seconds before she started assembling, in her mind, where flashlights and candles were. Then as quickly as the power had gone out, it was back on again, but not to *The Tonight Show*.

How odd, she thought as she listened to the voice of the newscaster discussing the protests for the Vietnam War. She pressed the button for another channel and saw young men in helmets, with rifles strapped across their shoulders, huddled close to the ground.

This, along with the curtains flapping wildly in the breeze, rain spattering onto the floor, and the sound of the wind beating the trees and slapping water against the little dock outside, paralyzed her for a moment. Naomi could only listen to the judder, judder of the images of young soldiers being carried on stretchers from the ground to the waiting choppers.

She got up and went to the window, her feet squishing into the wet carpet beneath, her body chilled as rain pelted against her. She pressed down on the window to shut it, and then she caught sight of the shadowy figure of someone in her yard, just this side of the dock. She called out angrily, "Hey you, what are you doing?" The figure ran toward the oak trees and out of sight and Naomi whispered, "Is that you Elmo?"

She heard Pitickity meowing loudly, his odd face looking up at her from the porch, and Naomi asked, "Who was it, Mr. Pitickity?"

The cat was wet, his eyes as always, shining and glowing in the glare of the porch light. He meowed again and Naomi reached for the telephone, then thought again about making a call to the police. It would take forever for them to get to her place. Instead, she pulled the small handgun from the bedside table and walked barefoot downstairs.

"What was that Mr. Bolton had said?" she whispered to herself. "Somebody has been stealing gas off of boats... *humph*. Well, honey, we ain't got no gas on our little boat. I haven't even taken the boat out since the last time Roy was on leave." She paused for a moment on the stairs and thought, *Roy*. She felt the pain in her heart and the chill of death. Her wet nightgown clinging to her, Naomi pushed her damp hair from her face, and she shook her head. "No. He is fine."

From the living room window, she could see the silhouette of the boat bobbing in the water. "I need to get it over to Swan Point Marina and get the bottom cleaned, it's been a few months. I bet there are barnacles all over the bottom."

Flipping the light switch, Naomi padded to the kitchen window. There was Pitickity rubbing against a post, his head turned toward her and his mouth wide as he caterwauled into the wet night air again and again.

"I swear you're ugly." She shook her head and with one hand against the gun in her robe pocket, opened the door. "Okay, Pitickity, I guess you can come in." Rubbing against Naomi's leg as he entered the kitchen, Pitickity's one glaring eye faded to normal, hazel green. He jumped to a cushioned kitchen chair and gazed at Naomi for a few moments, then gently began licking his paws and cleaning his face.

"Yes, somebody had you at one time. I do believe you are an abandoned house cat, left alone to fend for yourself." Naomi crouched down. "Who would do such a thing? Did your owner go off to war too?"

She grabbed a hand towel from the counter and, pulling the cat to her lap, gently rubbed against its fur. She could hear the loud purring. "Got your motor running, huh?" Naomi leaned closer and rubbed her fingers against the cat's neck.

"Are you really fifty years old? That's what Norwood and Mary say. They say they've seen you around here forever, but you're just looking for a home, aren't you Pitickity? How about some milk?" Naomi settled the cat on the floor and poured milk into a small bowl. Eyeing leftovers in the refrigerator, she reached for the fried shrimp she'd brought home from Riverview Restaurant and dropped a few into another bowl. "Here you go." Turning to leave, she peered out through the kitchen window again. She opened the door, walked outside, and hollered into the damp night air, "The gas can is empty! I have no money! I have a gun! Leave me alone so I don't have to use it!" She whispered, "Elmo? If that's you, you better stay away from me."

The skies had cleared and the rain had gone; her eyes perused the now clear skies. She saw the big dipper and the big W that made Cassiopeia. Certainly, Roy was seeing the constellations too, now. As she gazed in the cool night air, she could feel it. *He's not one of the men on a stretcher, he's either on the USS* Constellation *or in the air flying a mission. He would not be on the ground*, she reassured herself.

The night felt clean, like the little thunder storm had washed away all the bad thoughts she'd had earlier. She felt free and twirled on the lawn, her bare feet feeling, it seemed, all the blades of grass. Her arms wide, Naomi called out, "Oh, powers that be, love my man. I know, oh heavenly father, love my man as I do." Still twirling, feeling the wet grass against her feet and ankles, feeling the damp salt air on her skin, she knew all was right with Roy, that he was safe, that he was gazing at the stars at the very moment she was.

Pitickity had run back to her side and Naomi picked the cat up, hugging it to her chest as she walked back indoors. Before she could reach the top of the stairs, Pitickity jumped from her arms moved past her and skipped up the stairs as if he had been in the house before. She watched it slip into the doorway of her bedroom.

"This is freaky," Naomi laughed aloud, and followed. "Have you been here before?"

The cat mewed and jumped to the bed and to the pillow where Roy's head usually lay. Its claws kneading the fabric, Pitickity meowed again before curling into a ball.

Lifting the covers, Naomi slid onto her side of the bed. She could hear the cat's loud purring. Grinning, she let Norwood's fantastical story about the black cat drift through her brain, taking hold of the thoughts, embellishing them.

There was Roy as a little boy, petting Pitickity, sitting on the dock, fishing pole in hand. Running along the marsh, fishing in the river and motoring his little jon boat into the Intracoastal Waterway. There was the cat sitting on the dock watching it all.

Her attention turned to the singer now on the television, loudly crooning sad words, the melody rising and falling, the singer's face contorted as if in pain. Biting her lip, Naomi listened to the sad words and laid back against her pillow. Oh, how she missed Roy. It was a rollercoaster, one moment exuberant, knowing he was safe, the next moment swallowed whole by fear and worry. She closed her eyes and began a prayer. "Oh, heavenly father, please protect him …."

The gun, still in her robe pocket, felt uncomfortable and Naomi slid it out, laying it on the bed. She touched the metal, stroked the cool, smooth features and pushed it farther from her. "Keep him safe …." Juddering of choppers in the sky from nearby Camp Lejeune jolted her, erasing the prayer and the peace the prayer offered.

All the joy she'd felt about Roy's safety was completely gone, and she rushed to the window, parted the curtains, opened it and watched the helicopters as they moved southward. Her eyes searched the sky for the constellations. They were still there, offering hope and comfort once again.

Then Naomi watched the clouds move as if phantoms, slowly obscuring the stars. Little by little they moved, until finally the constellations could no longer be seen.

"What does this mean?" she asked herself aloud. She heard the cat meow, and turned to it, her face scowling. "I'm searching for omens, things to tell me the future, listening to crazy people, drinking crazy drinks, believing in pendants and black cats."

Her eyes continuing to search the sky, Naomi wondered just what she did believe in. It felt a sin to worry about Roy, to think he might never come home. How could that happen? He was so real, had been so much a part of her life, had made her life his. How could he go away? How could there never be Roy again?

Sitting cross-legged on the bed, she picked up the remote, turned back to the news, and raised the volume. The newscaster was still giving a summary of events that were happening in Vietnam. He turned to the monitor showing programming from earlier in the day. Naomi listened, leaned forward and petted Pitickity, who had come to nestle in her lap.

Three planes were shot down today over Tan Son Nhut in Vietnam. No word yet on casualties. Four wounded and two killed at a battle fifty miles north west of Saigon. Several women and children are said to have been killed during a bombing, while protesters in California performed a peaceful demonstration at the state capitol today. Naomi's eyes studied the footage of the protesters yelling as they pumped signs scrawled with the words, "Hell no we won't go!" And "Make love not war."

"My boyfriend was killed over there last month, there was no reason for him to be fighting for a place we know nothing about. Those people don't want us over there. This is an old man politician's war," a young woman shouted, her hair twisted with flowers and beads. A peace sign necklace hung from her neck as she spoke angrily into the microphone.

Her chest rising and falling as she thought, Naomi looked at the gun still laying on the bed. Had Roy been the one who had dropped the bombs on the women and children? Had he been in one of the planes shot down at that Tan-Son-*whatever* village? The names of the towns or villages, whatever they were called, all sounded the same and so unfamiliar.

Two boys from her graduating class had been killed. One had enlisted voluntarily, the other had been drafted. Most of the other males from her class and even some in grades ahead of and below her were either in the Marines or Navy. Some had opted for Army and some had been lucky enough to get in the National Guard. But they were all people she knew. Maybe not really well, but still, she knew them. They were real people. Were they dying, or dead? Were they killing innocent people?

Focusing on the young woman on television with the long blond braids, Naomi raised the volume. *We don't want any more of this war.* Naomi nodded her head. "I don't want any more of this war. I want Roy to come home, in one piece. I want my brother home. I want..."

Naomi thought of the drink Elmo had given her, of the words the clouds had spelled out. "Peace, love, sex." She said the words coolly, and recalled the initial high of whatever it was she had drunk and how wonderful it had felt.

It made sense to her, this sentiment the hippies expressed, and Naomi turned her head to the mirror and studied her reflection. She pulled her hair forward, parted it with her fingers and held up her fingers. "Peace baby." Laying on the bed partially listening to the television and partly to the words in her own head, things started to make sense and she picked up the phone book from her night stand.

"Ornell Curtain," she whispered, as her fingers slid down the list of surnames beginning with the letter C.

As far as she could remember, Ornell Curtain was Elmo's aunt.

CHAPTER 15

Should I get Roger something for Christmas? Mim mused. Counting the tips she had put away just for holiday gifts, she couldn't decide if having him over for Christmas was enough. According to her mother, it was. But Mim felt she should also get him a little something, if only to have a gift under the tree. Christmas just wasn't Christmas without at least one present.

Still, there had been no dates, no kissing or even holding hands. Theirs was a friendship. So far, Mim liked it that way. There were some days when she didn't see or hear from Roger at all; those were the times she assumed he was visiting one or more of his lady friends in Jacksonville. She'd come to understand that men needed that, whatever it was the lady friends were offering, and whatever it was, it was something she herself was not willing to surrender. Friendship would have to do. And as it grew, she realized that though she had married

Anthony and believed she loved him, they had never been friends.

Roger was still working on the Sneads Ferry job, though it seemed odd to her that marijuana-smoking Roger should be trying to catch marijuana dealers. But then, so much of the world seemed upside down, now. She decided that since they were just friends, his personal life was his and that she would be friends with the part she liked.

When he came to the island, they went fishing or crabbing and often ended up at the blue house where they talked about everything. Little by little, Roger divulged his history and now Mim knew what kind of home he had come from, and why he never went back. On occasion, he would even mention something about his time in Vietnam, about briefly meeting Kellie and the guy she was stuck on.

"You knew Larry?" Mim asked. "The guy Kellie was gaga over?"

"Yeah, we were like brothers over there."

"What happened?"

Quiet for a few moments, Roger began, "Everybody is different Mim. Larry couldn't take losing part of his body. Last I heard from him, he was still carrying the war around inside of him. We all do to some extent. It really took a toll on him, loosing part of his leg."

"What part?"

Roger chuckled, "The part that steals your soul." He smiled at her, then added, "It's funny, he lost half his leg, I lost my mind."

Mim understood to some extent. Hadn't Anthony stolen part of her soul when he'd beaten her and she'd lost their child?

She met his eyes. "You've moved on, haven't you?"

"Some days ... well, I'm working on it."

Pausing for a moment, she looked out to the winter ocean. Mim liked that time of year, when the wind was coming from a different direction and the sun seemed to lay across the ocean more softly. Everything was quieter, more peaceful and so different than summer time when tourists bombarded her home.

"It is beautiful here," she smiled gently to Roger.

"Yeah ... except when those damn choppers come across the sky." His lips turned downward as he inhaled a long breath. Sometimes, just the sound and it's ...." He flung his arms wide, thrusting his closed hands open. "It's freaky. But at the same time, it's a dose of what's really happening to me right now."

Mim wished she understood, and maybe she did partly; all she could surmise from her own experience with hell was that sometimes it just didn't go away. She nodded as Roger continued talking.

"I've been working on Larry, don't want to give up on him. He's a good man, but everybody has to fight their own battles."

Pulling her knees to her chest, Mim asked, "So, you are going to come over for Christmas dinner?"

"Thank you, I think I'd like that. But I'm helping at the VFW with Toys for Tots Saturday." He snickered lowly. "Jason is playing Santa Claus this year. Want to go there with me?"

It had been a while since she'd visited the VFW, not since Kellie had been home, and the thought of going, to her surprise, excited her. "Oh my gosh, I haven't even donated anything this year."

"It's not too late. Still a little over a week 'til Christmas and Santa's at the VFW day after tomorrow, so you have a couple of days."

"What do they need?"

He shrugged. "The boys like cap guns and tanks, the girls … baby dolls, I guess. Everybody likes transistor radios."

"And you're coming over for Christmas dinner. No Mr. Burger this time. Naomi is coming, Kellie's dad and brother Henry are coming too. So, it should be a lot of fun."

Roger nodded, and his eyes searched hers for a moment before he rose. "I got to get back to Jacksonville, Jason wants to talk with me."

Maybe he was telling her the truth, maybe he wasn't, but Mim had decided it wasn't her fight.

Whatever was going on with Roger, he had been right when he'd said that everybody had to fight his own battles. Hadn't she been fighting hers? Life with Anthony had changed her. Still, Mim wasn't sure how it had. One thing she knew for sure was that she shouldn't be rushing into a romance right now. So, it was perfect, a nice male friend, no expectations, no physical intimacy.

CHAPTER 16

Edna Myers placed a bowl into Roger's hand, the aroma filling his nostrils as he eyed the dark green contents.

"Collards," Edna grinned. "You had them at Thanksgiving. You like them, huh?"

He nodded and, balancing a bowl of mashed potatoes in his other hand, he turned toward the kitchen table.

"You know sweetie," Edna began, "I was so embarrassed about Amos Burger at Thanksgiving. I know his poor wife was, too. He just went on and on." Her eyes lifting to his, she grinned, "I just want to apologize and believe me, I won't be inviting him over for a while."

"Thank you, Mrs. Myers, but I'm used to blowhards. I just let those kinds of braggarts roll right off my back."

"And," Edna added, holding his gaze, "I know Mim and you are seeing each other, but I want you to know I'm not going to tolerate any hanky-panky. Do you understand?"

"We're friends, Mrs. Myers."

"Well, I know how young men think, that since she's been married ... if my husband were alive, he'd be having this talk with you--"

"I understand, Mrs. Myers."

"I'd like it very much if you'd call me Miss Edna. Everybody does."

"Yes ma'am, Miss Edna." Roger nodded as he walked to the table.

John Francis, seated at the head of the table, was already carving the turkey before him. He nodded to Roger. "This lady knows how to cook a Christmas dinner. I know of what I speak, I've been having Christmas dinners with her and her husband, Rufus, since I moved here and that's how many years Edna?"

"Twelve, fourteen, oh, I don't know. I know it's over ten ... since the girls were just kids playing in the dunes."

"Mutt and Jeff, those two," John added. "They were all over this island, playing in the marsh, and the warehouses, jumping out of those Bumble Bee towers. Two peas in a pod." His eyes held Roger's; there was no mistaking the stern tone as he began, "Mim and Kellie had a good upbringing here on the island."

Roger nodded, knowing exactly what John Francis meant.

"Mim tells me you knew Kellie in Nam."

"Yessir, but only briefly, while I was on the *Repose*. She's a fine girl, Mr. Francis, and very …. Well, I'll put it this way: she doesn't take any guff from anyone."

A quick, short nod from John as he continued carving the bird, and then he responded, "She's grown up alot since she enlisted. I'm glad she's doing well."

Edna seated herself at the opposite end of the table and folded her hands in her lap. "I am too. Kellie was always a good girl. Now," she said, "is everybody here? We need to begin the blessing before the food starts getting cold. She turned to Mim. "Isn't that friend of yours from Miller Motte coming?"

"She's supposed to, Momma."

"Well, we can't wait forever. We'll feed her when she gets here. We did say 3 p.m. sharp." Her eyes looked to the wall clock, then Edna grunted and added, "So everybody bow your heads."

"Blessed Heavenly Father," the prayer began to the slamming of a car door.

Lifting her head, Edna leaned just enough out of her chair to see Naomi walking hurriedly past a window.

Mim rose from the table, and opening the door, whispered, "You're late."

"I know," Naomi whispered back, and then more loudly, added, "I'm so sorry Miss Edna, I couldn't find Pitickity."

"Who?"

"Her cat," Roger groaned.

"Your cat?"

"Yes, ma'am. I wanted to leave him inside today, it's supposed to get cold later on." Naomi wrapped her arms around herself and shook, then giggled.

"I thought that's why they have fur," Henry guffawed as he watched Naomi move to the chair next to him. He eyed the paisley print mini-dress, the peace sign necklace and headband and chided, "Hippie now, huh?"

She slid a scornful glance his way.

"The peace sign is very groovy, Naomi." He leaned close as she sat down and whispered, "I bet I know what you've been smoking."

Naomi rolled her eyes. "Now you know, dear little Henry, that I've always been a fashion plate all my life and this is the latest fashion." Smoothing the front of her dress, she slid into the chair, adding, as she touched her long locks, "I'm in the groove, honey."

"If it walks like a duck," Henry sneered. "Hippie."

"Miss Edna, this all looks so good and the smell!" Lifting her head, Naomi closed her eyes and breathed deeply. "This is lovely, I'm going to write Roy about it."

"Hippie," Henry mocked again and, noticing her boots added, "These boots ... are they going to walk all over ... who?"

Naomi smiled innocently at Henry.

"Well, I think you look darling, my dear," interrupted Edna. "I'm glad you got here before we said the blessing." Nodding her head and waiting for the others to follow suit, Edna began again. "Blessed Heavenly Father, we thank You for these wonderful friends gathered here on Your day, and we ask that you keep us all safe from harm. Our futures rest in your hands, dear Lord. We ask for your guidance and to bless this food we are about to eat. In your name, Jesus Christ ...."

Henry called out *amen* and began reaching for the sweet potato casserole but was stopped by a sharp smack on the hand.

Edna's eyes pierced his. "And, dear Lord, we ask You to protect each and every one of us at this table. Help us to forgive one another and please give us the strength to fight our enemies abroad and in our own hearts. Bathe us with Your light and love so that we may prosper in this world full of chaos and sin and rise above to know You, our Lord." She paused, waiting for a second before adding, "Amen."

Roger reached for the bowl of collards. "Miss Edna, they smell so good I think I'll eat the whole bowl. He winked to Mim as he began filling his plate. He then studied Naomi's dress, noticing the pocket and the small piece of dark paper visible through the sheer fabric. Her eyes meeting his, Naomi grinned and slid the paper from the blouse pocket to her purse.

He knew instantly that Naomi was tripping. He recognized the colorful paper used for LSD and her dilated pupils. There was nothing he could do or say right now, so as he drifted in and out of conversations with the others, Roger kept his attention on Naomi, noticing how she picked at her food and rubbed her fingers, smiling as she did so. Whatever conversations she was having with others were short and she seemed more interested in smelling the food than eating it.

When she rose from the table, giggling, Naomi ran her fingertips over the embroidered flowers of the tablecloth. "Oh, Miss Edna, this is the most beautiful thing, it's so beautiful." She bent closer to the cloth. "The little flowers, oh, this is so … the colors …." Straightening, she giggled. "I have to be excused."

"Down the hall, second door on the right, past the kitchen," Mim called.

Waiting a few minutes, Roger rose and walked to the kitchen and waited for Naomi as she left the bathroom. "Having a nice trip, Naomi?"

"I'm coming down."

"You drove. I can't believe you drove all the way from Sneads Ferry like this.

"I'm coming down," she smiled up at him.

"Where did you get it?"

"Sunshine, it's just a little sunshine, Roger. And from what I understand, you like to smoke, what's the difference?" Naomi giggled loudly.

"Naomi?" Edna's voice called curiously, "If you go to the kitchen can you bring some more gravy, please?"

"Yes ma'am," she called back.

There was obviously something going on, Mim thought, as she watched Roger and Naomi find their seats at the table. Avoiding her gaze, she noticed him struggle to hide the scowl while he joined in conversation once again with John.

Naomi seemed giddy and then tired, alternating from one to another until she became complacent. They'd hardly spoken during the dinner, and as Mim tried to grab her friend's attention, Henry interrupted.

"Somebody lick the red off your candy?"

Naomi shook her head, her hair falling in her face as she lowered it. "I miss Roy. I hate the war, we've got no business …." She lifted her head, brushing the hair back from it, exposing her damp eyes. "I do like the cat though and I don't care what any of you think, I *do* think it's a magic cat." She smiled broadly, rose from her chair and, almost tripping, sat back down.

Mim had suspected it since Naomi had arrived. Now she was positive that Naomi must have been drinking. Studying her friend as she toyed with her food, it was obvious and, for a moment, Mim was angry. Then she recalled the conversation they'd had a few weeks ago, about Roy and the war and about how confused she was.

Naomi raised her head to study the table. Her eyes fell on Mim's and, recognizing the look, she shrugged her shoulders. Taking a bit of food, she slowly chewed, and turned her attention to the conversation between Roger and John. "I think I'm just going to go home now, Miss Edna. Thank you so much for the dinner." She rose again, this time steady on her feet.

"Do you think you should drive, dear?" Edna asked.

"I'm fine, really. And I'm not drunk, I know that's what you think Miss Edna, but it's not true. I just miss Roy and want things to go back to the way they used to be. In fact, I'm going to write his congressman." Moving the chair aside, she walked to the door. Roger rose and followed her outside, then returned moments later.

"She'll be fine." He reassured the others. "She's just … tired."

Roger slid a glance to Mim and smiled before resuming his conversation at the dinner table. Folding his arms on the table, he leaned forward and listened to the older man talk.

He's having a good time, Mim thought as she watched them talking. She was glad. *He's relaxed, he seems so … I don't know, like he's with people who understand him. Maybe he'll get it together.*

She liked Roger, always had, even when she thought he was just a surfer. And Mim liked that he was trying to move past what had happened in Vietnam, or at least cope with whatever demons he had.

But she didn't like that he did drugs. Was it true that pot was harmful, that it led to harder drugs? *What can I do about it if it does?*

Mim saw Henry flip a hand in the air, and watched as Roger and John laughed. *Must have been a joke*, she thought, Henry was always telling them. *They're all men, and men have this … like they're brothers or something.*

Going to the VFW with Kellie's family had always been fun, a little window into people from different parts of the country. The Toys for Tots party showed her once again another part of the world without having to actually leave the good old USA. They talked about Germany and Japan, and so many other places they had been.

Parents joined with the children to dance, and to help string popcorn for the tree. Then they played games until it was time to gather outside and watch Santa fly by in a helicopter, waving from the open bay. A few minutes later, he arrived by Kaiser military truck, one of the big ones that transported the men. Jason played Santa Claus, jolly and well padded, with his wife standing by as Mrs. Claus. Roger called out the names of the children and handed out gifts.

The Christmas event had been yet another example of the comradery of the military. It left her feeling as if she had been part of one huge family.

CHAPTER 17

April 1967

Elmo stepped from the fishing boat and waved as the paunchy, tanned driver backed the Chris-Craft ski boat from the slip. He waved to him and to the man's children sitting along the transom settee. His sunburned legs hurt as he walked, so did his arms. In fact, his whole body hurt from having lain on the beach at Lea Island nude.

"Thanks for picking me up," he called out as the boat motored slowly from the slip.

Brushing the long black strands of hair away from his face, Elmo pouted, his lips turning downward, his shoulders slumping as he ambled up the dock towards the dock house. *Why did they leave me behind?* He wondered, and thinking of how the four other young men on the skiff they'd taken to the island had invited him along, he pondered the question even more. *What did I do? They said they needed a dime bag. We were going to party at Lea Island.*

He'd never been there and the others, the ones he'd graduated Topsail High School with, had been eager for it to happen. They'd acted like old buddies, and they'd had the RC Cola and bottle of rum; they never did get to his pot.

The last thing he remembered was puking, running into the water and falling down in the sand. They'd all laughed, he'd laughed. "So, what did I do?" he asked aloud.

"Bunch of skuzz buckets, always have been. I'll get them back," he muttered as he opened the door to the phone booth. Wiping the sand from his tee-shirt, he added, "Lucky they left me my clothes." He reached into the back pocket and found the few coins left there, slipped a dime in the phone slot and waited for the ring.

"Hello? Naomi, I need a ride. I'm up here at the marina in Sloop Point, can you come pick me up?" He listened for a few moments, groaned a thanks and hung up the phone.

****

"What happened?" Naomi asked, while her eyes were focused on the winding, black top road. "You're as red as a beet."

"Real bummer, I fell asleep on Lea Island."

"Dummy, why did you do that?"

"I'm not a dummy," Elmo huffed, "I got taken, that's all. They filled me up with alcohol. Man, I can't drink alcohol, makes me sick and … and then I got drunk and the next thing I know, I'm lying on the sand, buck naked, scorched as hell."

"Who was it?"

"The usual ones, they never grew up. Said they wanted to get high and I have the stuff, you know that. But they had some rum and they got me drunk."

"They who?" Naomi pushed her long hair back across her shoulders.

"Norman, I remember him. He was always stuck up at school."

"No he wasn't, Elmo. he had a lisp and didn't like to talk with anyone because he got made fun of, but he wasn't stuck up."

"And Robert and John--the three of them. They got me drunk, took my clothes off me and left me there. I was really lucky when this ski boat came by and gave me a ride."

"Yes, you were lucky." Naomi thought of Norman. She'd known he always had a crush on her in high school. Hadn't he been the one who rode back with her Halloween night when Elmo had spiked her drink? "You better steer clear of those boys," she laughed.

Reaching into the back pocket of his shorts, Elmo pulled out his wallet. He held a small, thin tin in his hand and opened it to show Naomi the pills there.

"Where do you get all this stuff?" Naomi plucked a purple pill from the box. "What does it do?"

"Speed, man. You'll be typing two hundred words a minute on this shit," he laughed.

As she pulled into her driveway, Naomi popped the pill into her mouth and gulped loudly.

Elmo slammed the car door and, following her from a distance, trotted to the side of the house. "Hey, man you got an unreal view. Groovy, and you got a boat too." He moved back to catch up with Naomi as she slid the key into the door lock. "Cool, you have a boat. Are you going to take me out on it? Hey, you and me been groovin', you been smoking my dope and need to take me out on your boat. Just don't abandon me, hear that, chick?"

"I find it hard to believe that you, having grown up in Hampstead, never had a boat of your own. Why not?"

"My old man didn't like the water and my mom was always afraid I'd drown."

"Well, that could happen. Or you could get sunburned as all get out." Naomi laughed. "You did go to the beach, didn't you?"

"Like I said, my parents ...."

"You've always been weird, haven't you?" She shook her head as she went inside and, feeling a rush, she tittered softly, "So this is what speed feels like."

Elmo grinned, entered the home behind Naomi. Scanning the kitchen, he then wandered into the living room. "How about a tour of the house, Miss Priss?"

"You've seen most of it, not that much to see."

"What about the upstairs?" He ran his hands along the banister and moved slowly up the stairs.

"Just the bedroom and a few rooms Roy and I haven't completed yet. We worked on them when he was on leave last year." She raced past him on the stairs and giggled. "I'd love to see him right now."

"I bet you would," Elmo chuckled. "How do you like that little purple fellow I gave you? Kind of makes you long for it, huh?"

She turned, widening her eyes, and laughed. "Groovy ... this," she giggled, "is my bedroom. Actually, it's Roy's and my bedroom, but because he's halfway around the world, I'll call it Pitickity's bedroom." She nodded to the cat lazing on the bed. "Have you met Pitickity yet? Pitickity is the neighbor's cat or used to be the neighbor's cat but now it's my cat. I used to not like Pitickity, thought he was possessed or something, and my landlord says the cat is magic and used to be around fifty years ago, but I know that isn't true. He just looks like a lot of tom cats and since he's been fixed he's not really a tom cat anymore and ...." The words rolled wildly off her tongue as she watched Elmo pull a rolled marijuana cigarette from his back pocket.

He felt it to make sure it wasn't wet and thought how fortunate he was that, having been flung on the beach inside his pants, it wasn't. He flicked a lighter to the tip and inhaled deeply, holding the smoke inside as he extended the cigarette to Naomi.

"This will calm you down some," Elmo chuckled. Eyeing the radio on the night table, he bent to find a station. The heavy beat of a Creedence Clearwater song filled the room. Naomi closed her eyes to the sound and, holding the joint between her fingers, pressed it to her lips. Taking a small toke, she held it as she watched Elmo exhale slowly. She exhaled too and then took a longer draw on the joint before passing it back.

Naomi closed her eyes again to the enhanced sound of music. She fell back onto the bed, laying supine, drinking in the feeling consuming her body, engulfed in the dreamlike quality of the moment.

Elmo lay down beside her, his fingers gently stroking her arm. She sighed lightly, allowing him to move his hands along her thighs.

CHAPTER 18

Pitickity rubbed his body against Naomi's arm. His loud purring woke her to the darkness of the bedroom. Reaching to pet him, she pulled his furry body closer, and in doing so, realized her nakedness.

"Umm," she groaned, and sat upright, searching for her slippers with her feet. They were not there. Then she heard an audible fart, and for one split second thought of Roy, then glanced to the body on the side of the bed and recognized Elmo. His long, black, stringy hair lay twisted around his face. His thin form, lacking any definition, sprawled against the sheets and Naomi rose quickly, aghast as the recollection of what she'd done came to her.

She pulled her chenille robe from the hook inside the closet and wrapped herself before padding quickly to the bathroom. She closed the door softly and knelt at the toilet. Bile spewed along the porcelain sides. She thought again of the person lying in her bed and heaved a few more bits of bile into the bowl.

Wiping her mouth, Naomi pulled herself to the sink and splashed water on her face. She could hear the rousings of Elmo down the hall and heard him as he called out.

"Hey babe."

The endearment sent shivers across her skin and she sat on the commode, the robe still wrapped around her, her feet bare and cold and her head swimming with questions and anger. She got up and raced down the stairs to search the laundry room for clothing. A wrinkled pair of jeans and a top lay in the dirty clothes hamper. She decided they would do, and she dressed and ran outside.

He called several times while she hid in the work shed, and then finally as his voice rose, Naomi stepped outside. His face beamed as he walked toward her.

"You bastard," she called, "be quiet! How could you?"

Elmo stepped back, and still smiling, said, "You never said no, Naomi. In fact, you sure were acting like you loved it. You called me Roy. Do I remind you of Roy when I make love to you?"

She spat at him, "You bastard, get out of my sight! Get out before I call the cops!" She ran at him, her hands raised.

"Naomi, now what are the cops going to say when I tell them I spent the night?"

Her fists balled, and Naomi aimed for his face. His hand grabbed her wrist, but she easily overpowered him.

"You go to hell, you bastard! Get off my property." Her fist met his face and Elmo swayed before steadying himself. Wiping the blood from his nose, he turned and laughed. "You'll call me next time you want something."

"Go back to California, you creep."

Naomi went back inside and ran up to the bedroom. There, she pulled the nightstand table drawer out as far as it would go and pushed past the hair clips, aspirin bottle and other odds and ends until her hand found the packet of birth control pills.

"Damn," she cursed. *There was no need, Roy's been gone months.* Throwing the package across the room, she bit her lip. "I better not be." She thought of the hours before and what she'd allowed to happen and wiped her nose with the back of her hand. "I better not be, oh God, please don't let me be."

She studied the still-rumpled sheets for a moment before angrily tearing them from the bed and tossing them to the floor. The quilt, the one she loved so much, lay halfway on the floor too and Naomi jerked it to the floor as well. She kicked the bundle of linens down the hall, then watched as they rolled down the stairs in a heap. Pushing with her feet, she moved it all toward the laundry room.

"Hell no, these need burned," she growled. Opening the back door, she pushed the bundle of bed linens outside.

****

With her legs crossed, Naomi had slumped back in the lawn chair; she watched as the pile of sheets was quickly consumed by the fire. Throwing an oak branch onto the flames, she listened to the crackle of fire and watched as flames licked the night sky.

The stars were out, and she could see the constellations perfectly, but there was no welling in her heart for Roy. He seemed farther away than ever. Not just in a different country, but in a different part of her. He was a dream now, someone from the past. Still, she felt she owed him some kind of loyalty, at least to their marriage.

She longed for the ache that had faded over the last few months.

"I've screwed everything up," she said aloud, and thought for a moment how nice a joint would be now.

Rolling her eyes, Naomi spit, "I've really screwed things up." Pitickity purred as he rubbed against the lawn chair, his one eye glaring with the flames and the other dull and milky.

"You're ugly as hell. You do look like a devil cat."

Pitickity mewed softly again and jumped to Naomi's lap. He lay curled there, purring, his warm body competing with the warmth of the fire. Naomi's hand slid softly against the cat's fur. "Sorry boy, I don't mean anything by that, you're not a devil cat, or a magic cat, you're just a plain old cat and you can't help being ugly no more than Roy can help that I don't love him anymore."

The words startled her and she felt her belly. "Is there a little Elmo in there? Pitickity, use your magic and make it go away." She closed her eyes again, losing herself in prayer only to be startled by the sound of deep laughter and tittering. *Norwood and Mary. Oh shit, I don't need them coming around now.* Naomi turned, and raised her lips in a welcoming grin.

"Hi."

"We were out for our nightly constitutional and smelled the smoke and wondered if you might be having a weenie roast out here," Norwood Bolton chuckled.

"I've got some chicken legs in the fridge if you want to add anything," Mary Bolton offered.

"No, no. I've already eaten my dinner. The cat upchucked on the sheets and I decided to have a bonfire."

"Sheets? You're burning sheets?" Mary queried. "Oh honey, sheets are so expensive, a little stain wouldn't have hurt anything."

Naomi shrugged, "Well, they're gone now." She turned back to gaze into the fire.

Gently placing her hand on Naomi's left shoulder, Mary asked if she'd heard from her husband lately.

"Uh-uh. Been about a week, but that's not unusual." Naomi tensed as she felt Norwood standing on her right.

"I noticed some hippie-looking man hanging around here, guess he's a friend of yours, huh?"

"Not really," Naomi stood, her back to the couple as she moved toward the dock. "I went to school with him. He's just some bum now, I don't know why he came over to my house." She folded her arms as she walked further toward the dock. "I'm really kind of tired right now, if you don't mind." Turning to face the couple, Naomi cocked her head to the side a bit. "I'm getting ready to go to bed."

"Um," Mary Bolton began, "well, if there's anything I can do for you, let me know."

"If that bum comes around here bothering you anymore, just call me. I've got a .22 that will take care of that." His arms at his side, Norwood furrowed his brow. "I'll watch out for you." Chuckling, he added, "I see you've made old Pitickity yours. I wouldn't think the neighbors would mind, after all, they were just feeding it. I don't think it really belonged to them. I don't think that cat has ever belonged to anybody. Why when I was a kid, he didn't ...."

"Mr. Bolton, I'm really tired," Naomi snapped.

Mary threaded her arm through Norwood's. "Come on dearie, the child is tired." She stepped a few feet and said, "The pendant. I know something is amiss, my dear. Ponder the pendant. It has powers too."

Naomi didn't answer, but turned back toward the water, and as she neared the wooden structure, she scoffed, whispering, "Damn magic cat, magic pendant, magic constellations in the sky. It's all bullshit."

She felt numb, cold and unable to focus on anything besides the possibility that she may have become pregnant and how stupid she had been. Entering her room, she watched Pitickity jump from the floor to the bed, immediately finding Roy's pillow and kneading it with his claws.

"Omens, omens, what is the cat telling me now?" She looked at the bare bed and thought of the task of making it. "I hate making the bed," she scoffed, then turned to the hallway and selected the yellow sheets from the linen closet.

"Scat cat." Naomi flicked her hand toward the cat as she flapped the sheet in the air. It billowed out almost perfectly above the mattress.

Folding the corners beneath the top mattress, she pulled tightly to erase any wrinkles there might have been. She flapped another sheet in the air, and it too billowed above the bed and Naomi waited for it to settle atop the other. And then she spied the half-smoked joint in the ashtray, partially hidden behind the lamp. "Ah, look what Elmo the idiot left." She looked closer by the lamp and found that he'd left his wallet and a small vial. She opened the lid and poured out an assortment of colored pills and a small bag of marijuana. Scooping it all into the drawer of the bedside table, she finished making the bed.

CHAPTER 19

It was now eight days past the time her period was due and three weeks since she'd been with Elmo. Naomi thought of the old wives' tales, the ones that would help her abort a baby, if she had one inside her. Cinnamon and papaya were supposed to work if taken in large amounts. So was massaging her abdomen and taking hot showers. Naomi recalled a girl in high school who had mentioned that she had used her father's weights and exercised radically until she'd bled.

She thought of anything that could make her get rid of what might be growing inside her and wondered about the sin of it.

Mary Bolton had stopped by the day before, offering sympathy for the lost bedding. She had dropped a little innuendo about the hippie boy she'd seen, asking if there was trouble with him. Naomi wondered if Mary knew more than she let on. She wondered if the Boltons would kick her out of their house if she was pregnant?

Certainly, Roy would want a divorce. Even if she was not pregnant, he would want one when he found out about Elmo. Naomi knew that at some point she would tell him about that. They had never kept secrets, but writing to him about it now wasn't right either. Nodding her head, she decided to try the remedies. She'd start with the hot showers and then try the cinnamon.

Startled by the sound of a horn blaring, Naomi rushed to the window. Lenore, her mother-in-law grinned up at her, her eyes belying any happiness to see her.

She rolled the car window down and shouted, "Come down here, I have something for you and I don't want to get out of the car. Come on now, hurry!"

That was Lenore, always wanting things her way, demanding attention immediately. Naomi shooed Pitickity from the bed and quickly pulled the sheets up. "Her majesty might want to come inside," Naomi smirked as she slid her flip flops on. "Wonder what the old bag of worms wants now? I suppose she wants to give me notes on how to keep a clean house or what I need to do with my hair."

Quickly making her way towards the staircase, Naomi felt fur at her ankles as Pitickity wound between her legs, tripping her as she stepped.

Naomi caught herself, gave the cat an admonishing look and continued more slowly down the staircase.

She heard the car's horn blare again, and her mother-in-law's voice.

"Yes, Mrs. Simpson, I'm here, I nearly fell down the stairs trying to hurry."

"That should teach you. If you'd pace yourself, you wouldn't have accidents, my dear. But honey," she offered snidely as she reached her arm from the window. Waving a small brown package, she said, "I like it best when you call me Lenore. Okay, honey?" She raised a brow, and added, "I thought you might be able to use this, I noticed that you've been putting on a little weight and I saw this at Belks."

Naomi met her eyes. "How thoughtful of you, *honey*."

"Oh dear, sarcasm doesn't look nice on you," Lenore tittered. "I'd come in but I'm sure you're busy cleaning. Try to tidy up your hair, dear, it looks like a rat's nest."

Naomi stood there, dumbstruck, wanting to scratch the older woman's eyes out, but lacking the right words to suggest the idea.

"Ta ta," Lenore gunned the big Cadillac and pulled from the driveway. "Behave yourself now," she added loudly.

Behave myself? Why should she think I'm not? Has someone told her that Elmo was here? Did someone see him leave my house? Naomi's heart beat fast and she swooned for a moment, thinking of the baby that might be forming inside her.

In her bedroom, Naomi sat on the bed, and tore slowly at the wrapped package she'd been given. She thought of how the cat had almost made her fall down the stairs. *Wouldn't that have done it?* she thought. *Wouldn't that have caused a miscarriage?*

The garment fell to the floor. Naomi picked it up and, holding before her, shook out the wrinkles. She liked the color and the print: stars and moons in yellow and pale blue. The romper was cute; she wondered if Lenore could be having a change of heart, but quickly dismissed the idea as she remembered the snide remarks and snarky attitude of her mother-in-law.

Her fingers felt the padded bra built into the top of the romper, and considered that perhaps Lenore was being thoughtful. Stepping into it, she squeezed the material to her hips, barely bringing the romper past them and to her waist. The top with the padding would do, but the bottom was too small. Checking the tag, she read, *irregular.* "You old biddy, you knew what you were doing. You did it on purpose."

Reaching into the drawer, she rifled through the pills she'd put there a few weeks ago and plucked out a blue pill. "I'll lose the weight you bitch and I'll flaunt it." Holding the pill between her fingers, Naomi raised it to her lips. "Oh, the baby," she whispered, reconsidering. She took aim at the trash can across the room, and lobbed the pill into it. "Two points," she laughed.

****

Mim glanced toward Naomi, who was seated halfway through the first row of desks, and noticed her shoulders, and the somewhat wrinkled blouse covering them. It was so unlike Naomi to dress so untidily. She noticed, too, how Naomi had been letting her hair grow, and how it now hung now past her shoulders, unruly and lackluster.

Naomi had never been one to ignore her appearance, and Mim wondered if there had been any news about Roy. Was he okay, was their relationship still good? One of the girls she knew had received a letter from her boyfriend that he was breaking it off; he was in love with a Vietnamese girl. Maybe something like that had happened with Roy. The nightly news had been horrible. The war was horrible, ongoing with casualties, always casualties and it seemed it would go on forever. Maybe Roy had been injured, or worse.

Whatever it was, Naomi was not talking.

Mim thought of Kellie and the letters she'd been receiving from her, mostly filled with routine tasks, rarely anything personal, except for the times she took R and R at Cameron Bay. The last correspondence Mim had received from her friend had been a package containing a silk blouse and an enclosed letter mentioning that Kellie had received a letter from Larry, the Marine she'd fallen in love with early on in her tour of duty.

Sometimes he seems like a dream I had. Kellie had written, *it seems so long ago and there have been so many others who have come and gone.*

"Sometimes Anthony seems like a dream I had, a bad one," Mim whispered to herself. So much had changed, even in the time since she'd come back from Detroit. People with whom she'd had relationships had changed, so much so that she wondered if she really ever known them at all.

Turning her attention back to the instructor, Mim listened to the monotone delivery of information. She'd become bored with the most recent etiquette assignments and felt it was *so* outdated. Leaning her chin against the palms of her hands, she looked at the instructor, watched her mouth move and then slowly let her attention drift to the tree outside the window of the classroom.

Mim watched a bird jump from limb to limb. She watched for several moments, the voice of the instructor becoming more background noise. She glanced once more to Naomi. Obviously, she was bored too, and their eyes met.

Surprised by the smile she offered, Mim nodded and gestured for them to meet after class.

* * * *

"So, when are we going to Cherry Point again?" Mim asked. "I need some excitement in my life and it's been a while. I haven't seen much of you. Is everything okay?"

Naomi shrugged. "I guess, been busy."

"Is Roy alright?"

"Why wouldn't he be?"

Taken aback by Naomi's response, Mim snapped back, "Look, I thought we were friends, but now I'm afraid to talk to you and you're acting like your snobby old self."

Naomi sighed, "I don't know anymore." Her eyes searched Mim's. "I'm sorry, yes, we're still friends." She reached her hand out to touch Mim's hand. "Okay, let's go to Cherry Point, if you want to. I need some fun before I can't have any at all."

She didn't know how to take the last statement, but Mim took what she could get, thinking that maybe on the way to the dance, she'd get more information.

And she did.

Naomi stood waiting outside her house, dressed in a paisley print baby doll dress and white, strappy sandals. She slid into the passenger seat of the blue Mustang Mim had driven, turned her head and said, "I'm going to get drunk on my ass, one last time."

"So that's why I'm driving."

"Mm-hmm, I'm letting it all hang out tonight."

Mim backed from the driveway, hoping to hear a reason for the changes in Naomi's appearance or information about her life, anything that could explain the weight loss and attitude. But all the way up highway 210 Naomi was quiet as she fiddled with the radio dial. Then from out of nowhere she burst out, "I'm going to ask Roy for a divorce."

"No!" The word burst from Mim's mouth. "Why, Naomi? Is he seeing one of those Vietnamese girls?"

Naomi shook her head. "Well, I don't know for sure. Maybe he is, for all I know. But I just don't want to be married anymore and I think I'm going to move away, at least for a while. Think I'll move to Texas or Florida, somewhere where there is lots of space."

"This is kind of all of a sudden, Naomi. What's going on? I know things are changing, I can see you've lost a lot of weight and--"

Naomi reached inside her purse and pulled a joint from the folds of her wallet. She brought the lighter to the tip and lit it, then pulled heavily, holding the inhale for several seconds.

"Damnit, I knew it was pot or something. Some kind of drugs! Look, I'm not going to jail with you. Get rid of that. Now!"

Pulling on the joint, Naomi shook her head no.

"I just knew it. Ever since Christmas, I knew you were drunk or something then. Why Naomi? Why are you doing this now? It's so unlike you."

Naomi shrugged and exhaled.

"And you don't call or even answer your phone hardly at all. And you've missed some days at college. What's up?"

"Things change, I've changed." Naomi slumped down in the bucket seat of the Mustang.

"What is it with you and Roger? He smokes that stuff too."

"You should try it, Mim. It won't hurt you. It's like getting drunk without the hangover."

"I kind of understand Roger, he's been in Vietnam, seen hell, but you Naomi? What the hell, you've got everything, I mean everything. Why are you...?"

Naomi leaned her head against the headrest and closed her eyes, speaking calmly as she rubbed her stomach. "Don't get all bummed out."

"We're going back home," Mim slowed the car, watching as Naomi inhaled again. "You're such an idiot."

"I know, I've ruined everything, but I don't care anymore. It just doesn't matter anymore."

Mim pulled into the A&W drive-in restaurant, and watched the girl in the brown and orange skirt come to her car.

"Two root beers and an order of French fries."

The waitress nodded and walked back to the main building, returning a few minutes later with a tray of drinks and the fries. Mim rolled the window to half way, and the waitress rested it there before walking away.

"What's going on?"

"I'm pregnant."

Pausing for a moment, Mim asked, "Are you sure?"

Naomi shrugged. "I missed my period. I never miss my period."

"Well, you look like shit. "Who ...?"

"I don't want a baby."

"Is that why you're going to Texas ... or Florida ... some place big with lots of space?" Mim added sarcastically.

"I can have it then come back home ... maybe."

"And what about your husband?"

"I've screwed everything up. Lord knows, Roy will hate me. His mother will tell the whole town, the whole state. My family, they already hate me."

Mim shook her head, "I'm sorry your folks are the way--"

"Just because we didn't go to college, just because we loved each other and wanted to live our lives the way we wanted to. You'd think we burned the church down or something." Naomi turned her head towards Mim, her hand wiping away tears. "You know, they never call. They never come visit or ask me to and my mother is so controlled … she's scared of my father. Did you know that Mim?"

Mim looked at the marijuana cigarette Naomi held by her side. "You know that shit stinks, don't you? You're going to get me arrested and put in jail." Her voice rose as she started the car. Noticing the waitress peering from the window, Mim reached into her purse and set a dollar and some change on the tray. "I'm truly sorry about your parents, Naomi. I think it's horrible the way--"

Naomi rolled her head to the side, her eyes soft and begging, and asked, "Are we still going to Cherry Point?"

"Only if you get rid of that thing," Mim nodded to the joint.

Rounding the curb to highway 17, Naomi rolled the window down and tossed it.

True to her word, Naomi got drunk that night at the dance. Refusing to slow dance with anyone, she acted the fool as she bounced around the dance floor, dancing the jerk and the swim. Mim watched from their table or when she accepted a stranger's request, wondering the whole while if she'd done the right thing by coming to Cherry Point.

To her surprise, around eleven o'clock Naomi asked if they could leave. The young man holding her hand pleaded for her to stay, but she was adamant and kissed him on the cheek. "I'm married, sugar pie."

"I don't care," he followed.

Like so many things in her life that had happened, the events of that evening seemed to happen all at once. Time didn't seem to exist and if she could have stood back and looked at the clock of her life, Mim would have been amazed that the death of her father, her relationship with Anthony and its demise, falling for Roger and the ongoing Vietnam War had all happened in the space of four years. Her hemline had gone from middle knee to middle thigh, her lipstick from red to light pink and beliefs from conservative to not-so-sure. She'd thrown out the hats and gloves, the crinolines, and the garter belt.

Times were changing, and as Naomi left the bar, *drunk on her ass* as promised, she shouted as she pulled her bra from beneath her blouse. "I'm burning this thing as soon as I get home!" She laughed, stepped a few feet away from the car, leaned over to vomit and was struck by a car speeding through the parking lot.

CHAPTER 20

"No need to go to any far-off places now," Mim glowered at Naomi as she softly touched her hand.

"Just lucky I guess," Naomi replied, pulling the sheet closer to her chin and touching the tube leading from her hand to the drip. Thanks for being here."

"Your mother and father are on the way. So are Roy's parents."

Naomi rolled her eyes. "This should be fun."

Dr. Franklin stood at the foot of the bed perusing the medical chart. "Yes, you were lucky little lady," the doctor sneered, lifting his eyes towards Naomi. "Could we talk privately?"

"Mim is my friend, doctor."

"Your privacy, your decision, not mine. Well ... mild pelvic fracture, but you did lose a lot of blood ... a *lot*." He looked at her and raised a brow "And you lost the baby." He raised his judgmental eyes to hers. "Any questions?"

"No … please."

He looked sternly at her for a moment. "If you were my daughter …." he raised a brow, then turned back to the chart.

Naomi lowered her eyes and brought her hand to shield her face. "Please do not say anything to my parents."

The doctor shook his head. "You're over twenty-one, Mrs. Simpson." He paused for a moment, looked from Naomi to Mim and added, "You can go home in a couple of days. You will need crutches or a walker and someone to help you. Do you have someone?"

* * * *

Adele Cartwright gently pushed the door open and looked at her daughter as she slept. Tip-toeing next to her bed, she sat in the bedside chair and folded her gloved hands in her lap. "My baby," she whispered.

Naomi's eyes opened and, returning her mother's smile, she whispered too, "Sorry Momma."

"I'm sorry darlin'. I should have been here for you. I shouldn't have let you be so alone in that old house in Sneads Ferry." She clasped her daughter's hand. "I let my pride get in the way."

"I'm going to Miller Motte, Momma."

Adele's eyes brightened. "That's wonderful darlin', I heard you were." She paused for a moment to stifle a sob. "I hope that Roy is okay in Vietnam. You know I pray for you every night."

"Where's Daddy? Does he know you're here?"

"Oh," Adele began, "he's out of town on business. You know how busy he gets this time of the year."

Naomi rolled her eyes. "Busy my butt, he's out messing around Momma and you know it." She turned her head away for a moment. "Momma you need to leave Daddy, he's tearing you apart."

Withdrawing her hand from her daughter's, Adele pulled back from the bedside railing. "He wouldn't know what to do without me, sweetie."

Shaking her head, Naomi sighed and reached out for her mother's hand. "Momma, I know the reason you haven't called or come by is because of him. I know it's not your pride, it's his, and he forbade you to. I know, don't blame yourself."

Adele Cartwright folded one gloved hand over the other, and rubbed her lips together. "He can't help who he is, Naomi. I always forgive him." Lifting her head, she smiled softly and added, "I have driven by your house at night, or rather early mornings when he's gone out of town. You have a lovely yard. You're making it so pretty."

"Did you try to call him? Did he tell you where he's at?

Pausing, Adele answered, "Georgia, at the Sheraton in Atlanta. He didn't answer but I left a message for him. Now, let's not talk about that. I want you to tell me about your house."

"Oh Momma, I wish …."

Adele leaned in again. "It's okay darlin', he's who he is and God help me, I love him. And I bet you that once he hears that you're in the hospital he'll come see you."

"I don't want him to come see me. I don't want to see him. He's such a bully."

"He just wants the best for you, Naomi. That's all."

"He wants what *he* wants for me. He doesn't give a damn about me or for you Momma, or he wouldn't have--"

"Now, don't get yourself upset, darlin'".

"Okay." Naomi smiled and took a deep breath. "How's that? I'm calm now, okay? So, you like my flower garden?"

"Yes, it's lovely. You've put a lot of work into it. I can tell."

"How did you find out about me, Momma?"

"That little girl from Surf City came over."

"Mim."

Adele nodded. "She seems like a nice girl. She said she goes to school with you at Miller Motte.

She told me you and her went to Cherry Point to a dance club or something like that. Why would you go to a dance club, darlin', you're a married woman?"

"It's not like that, Momma. I haven't done anything--" Naomi caught her breath. "I just go to the club to dance. It gets my mind off of Roy and that damn war. But I don't flirt with the Marines there. I just have fun and I always go with Mim or somebody. They watch out for me."

Her hand caressing her daughter's brow, Adele bit her lip. "I worry so much about your brother Harold. You know he's in that war and ... he's my baby." Her eyes lifted to meet Naomi's, begging for compassion.

It had always been that way, *her baby Harold*. Yes, Naomi loved her brother, but he had never done anything wrong in her mother's eyes, and nothing right in her father's.

"I pray for him every night, Momma. Harold will be fine. He's smart."

Adele nodded, grinned and wiped her eyes. "I'm sure he is, dear. I get letters ... well, *you* should come to me if anything is wrong. About Roy ... or any other boys ... or anything, my dear. I understand the way things are a lot more than you think I do. I was young once." Adele pressed her lips together. "I remember being your age and being in love and how hard things can be. You know, your daddy was in Europe for a long time during World War II. I know the lonely feelings."

Naomi studied her mother's face. She knew how hard it was for her to disobey her husband and how he bullied her. She looked for signs of bruising, first on her mother's face, then her arms. A thin, long-sleeved blouse covered her slender limbs.

"It's hot outside Momma, why the long sleeves and gloves?"

"A lady always wears gloves, darlin', you know that."

Both turned toward the nurse entering the room.

"Is it time for me to go?" Adele asked.

"Visiting hours are over. Next time try to get here earlier."

"Oh, I think they're letting me go in a few days, Momma. You better stay home. I don't want you to ...."

Adele grasped her daughter's hand, stood and kissed Naomi's forehead. "I'll be just fine. I'll try to visit and--"

"Roy's mother is coming to stay with me for a while."

"Wonderful, I won't worry so much."

Leaning again to kiss her daughter's forehead, Adele slowly walked toward the door. Turning before shutting it, she blew a kiss and mouthed the words, *I love you*.

You marry that fisherman and I'll disown you. The words of Jerome Cartwright, her father, echoed in Naomi's head as she recalled the scene. Her father yelling, her mother cowering beside him. Part of her had wanted her mother to stand up for her, to stand up to her husband, but the price for doing so had been too high, and Naomi had shaken her head as Adele had risen from her chair.

A quick glance from Jerry had conveyed the warning and Adele had returned to her seat. Naomi knew her father meant what he'd said. She knew the look and she knew how cruel and controlling he was. He had even written off Harold when he'd enlisted in the Marines.

"You can wipe my ass, old man," Harold had said before slamming the door. Harold had slid a glance to Naomi too that day, a glance of kinship, love and shared dislike for their father.

She had not heard from him in two years, though she'd heard from friends that had received letters, and he was well.

Naomi had not heard from her parents either since she and Roy had married, except for the times she and her mother had met at Belk Berry in Wilmington. But there had been consequences to the second meeting when a neighbor had seen them together.

There would be no more communication between them after that, no phone calls, no letters.

CHAPTER 21

"I need you to do something for me, no questions asked."

Mim held the phone to her ear and listened as Naomi explained.

"I don't need any judgmental *I told you so's* or any feeling sorry for me, because I surely don't deserve that. I just need you to do this thing for me, Mim. You're the only friend I have that I can trust to do this."

"Anything, as long as it's not illegal," Mim tittered, then heard the silence from the other end. "Oh ... I'll try, Naomi. You don't want me to go get you anything, do you?"

"I want you to go to my house and go upstairs to my bedroom. Open the drawer in the bedside table nearest the window and you will see a bunch of pills and a small bag of grass. I want you to take all of those things and flush them down the commode."

"Umm ...."

"What is it? Please Mim. I need you to do this for me. My mother-in-law ...."

"You've been acting so weird lately, I thought something was going on with you. Naomi. Why in the world--"

"I said no questions, please Mim. I'm sorry. Sometime soon I'll explain things to you. But please, please do this for me. I'm coming home and my mother-in-law is going to be there *taking care of me.* Damn, I hate it, but she *volunteered* and I know she can't wait for the chance to get in my house and snoop around. Who knows what she writes to Roy?"

Naomi could hear her friend's breath through the phone. She waited. "Please Mim. I was messed up. Please Mim."

"I know what it's like to be messed up," Mim began, "well, not on marijuana and pills, but you know, messed up."

"Well, okay, you'll do it, then?"

"Okay."

"And change the flowers, I'm sure they need sprucing up. Just take some daises and peonies out of my garden, the one in the backyard. Okay?"

"Okay, but how do I get in?"

"And Mim, Mrs. Bolton is coming over to fix a place for me in the dining room. Let her in, okay?"

"Okay."

"And don't forget the flowers! Thanks so much, Mim."

Mim lifted the third potted petunia on the right and palmed the house key. She looked left and right, searching for someone watching, dismissing the reassurance from Naomi that it would be fine for her to enter her home.

Closing the door gently behind her, Mim noticed the vase of flowers on the dining room table and noted that she would change them before leaving. She took the stairs slowly and turned left at the top, as Naomi had instructed.

"She was right, the place is a mess up here." She eyed the paint cans and brushes lined along the hallway floor and the drop cloths bunched around them. "Mrs. High and Mighty isn't going to like that, either." She made another mental note to clear the hallway before she left.

As Naomi had instructed, Mim took off her shoes before entering the bedroom. Her feet felt the softness of the thick shag carpeting and her nose caught the instant scent of flowers. Perusing the room for a vase, she found none, but she noticed instead the round tins of sachet placed here and there. She walked to the window, opened it slightly and let the breeze blow the white lace curtains softly away from the sill, then smoothed the quilt on the bed and hung up the robe draped across the vanity chair.

Running a finger along the top of the Zenith television, Mim recalled Naomi mentioning that it was a color set. "Must be nice," she cooed as she picked up the remote control. She'd never seen a television with a remote and backing to sit on the edge of the bed, Mim pressed the *on* button. Slowly, the gray screen burst into life with the notable NBC peacock spreading its tail of colors. She looked at her wristwatch. "Exactly 11:30."

Her lips lifted as the announcer began. *The Hollywood Squares, with your host Peter Marshall!* The camera closed in on Wally Cox, Rose Marie, Buddy Hackett, Paul Lynde, and others. It was the first time she'd seen a show in color and for a moment she lost herself in the excitement of it all.

A Mr. Clean commercial roused her to remembering what she had come there for and she opened the drawer to the bedside table and found the bag of marijuana and several colored pills. She swept them all into her hand and walked briskly to the bathroom and shook the weed out of the plastic sandwich bag into the commode. She opened her fist and let the pills plop into the water as well, then flushed it all, waiting to make sure everything had gone down the drain.

Stuffing the empty plastic bag into her jeans, Mim walked back into the bedroom and rested once again on the end of the bed. She pressed a button once more to find the CBS station and then again to find ABC. "Sometimes UHF," she said as she flipped there, only to find the picture fuzzy. She clicked back to NBC and *Hollywood Squares*, laughed at one of the remarks to a question and smiled as she clicked the set off. "Neato," Mim tittered as she looked at her watch. "Naomi should be here around 2 p.m., plenty of time to put new flowers in the vase."

Glancing to the dried and wilted ones there now, she caught an older woman peering through the window. *She's early!* Mim thought, while racing to the door. "Hi Mrs. Bolton. Naomi said you would be here to help make the bed."

"Call me Mary, honey. And I brought an old bedspread I haven't been using, too." She moved past Mim. "I've seen your car here before. Aren't you the friend from Topsail who gives her a ride to school now and then?"

Mim nodded, "Naomi was in a little accident."

"Well, I knew about that. Naomi called us, and my husband is picking her up today and bringing her home. Do you know who is going to stay with her and help her? I know that child is going to need help for at least a week or more."

"Naomi's mother-in-law is coming to help her."

"Oh my gosh, that poor girl. Her mother-in-law is going to drive her crazy."

Mim curled a lip. "I know. I offered to help, but I guess it's Lenore."

"That--that woman," Mary stammered as she shook her head. "Mean as a snake." Touching Mim's arm she leaned in and said, "I know stuff about that woman, bad, mean, and selfish ...."

"Well," Mim began, not wanting to hear the gossip about Naomi's family, "I guess you know where things are here in the house."

Mary took the stairs briskly, returning within a few minutes with an armload of bed linens. "I'll make the couch and she can have this bedspread; I don't use it anymore and since she burned hers--"

"Burned her bedspread?"

"I'm sure she had a good reason. I think it was something about the cat." Mary tapped the side of her head. "Oh, yes, Naomi asked me to feed the cat. She said she had some cans of cat food in the cupboard. Can you take care of that, dear? I want to go ahead and make the bed before she gets home."

It was as if a whirling breeze had come into the living area of Naomi's downstairs, since it seemed that within minutes of her arrival, she had made the couch up for a bed, dusted the furniture and opened the curtains. "Don't forget the flowers in the dining room, Mim. Naomi says if there ain't fresh flowers in the vase, Lenore will have a fit. That's one *House Beautiful* woman now, but I have to run, Mim. It was nice to finally meet you. And if you can, be sure to have Naomi--well, if she doesn't have the pendant with her, then remind her to bring it downstairs. It will bring her calmness and good things."

Well, that was strange, Mim thought, as Mary left. She filled a small dish with cat food and watched as Pitickity jogged across the lawn. It was as if he knew it was time for dinner. "Things are odd around here. I thought my life was messed up … and you Mr. Pitickity, you were just about homeless."

Mim thought of the day Naomi had brought the cat to the island, the day she was going to leave it there, and she thought of how ordinary her life was without pendants and cats and nosy neighbors. And how dull it was without a husband, or even a potential one.

Sauntering to the window facing the river, Mim watched as two shrimp trawlers made their way south. *Naomi has a beautiful view, she* thought as she settled herself in a chair facing the backyard. She relaxed for a few moments, perusing the slow-moving water, the dock leading out to the little pier and the boat tied there, gently rocking in the wake of the larger trawlers.

Her eyes wandered to the flower garden nestled between the back of the house and a small shed. It was smaller than the one Naomi had in the front, but it had only two types of flowers: daises and peonies. "Vase flowers," Mim spoke as she rose to grab the vase from the dining room table. "Can't forget the flowers."

CHAPTER 22

Lenore Simpson walked through the house to the backyard of her son and daughter-in-law's home and, making herself comfortable on the patio settee, folded her arms across her chest. She looked across the broad waters at the buildings of Court House Bay and thought of Corporal Lorran and the last time they'd been together.

Closing her eyes, she leaned back and daydreamed about Dillon Lorran, of how strong and commanding he looked in his uniform. "Oh, baby," she cooed aloud, "you just wait." Lost in his arms, she barely heard the sound of a car pulling up outside the house. Immediately, she jumped to smooth the new ensemble Dillon had purchased for her during the last trip to Raleigh, and rushed to the front door.

"Oh." Norwood Bolton said, as he stuffed the key into his trousers when Lenore opened the front door. "Thought you'd be around back."

Lenore nodded. "It is my son's house and I do have a key." Her eyes slid from Norwood to Naomi. "She's still in the car, huh?"

"She has a little problem with mobility, Lenore. She *was* hit by a car, you know."

Lenore curled her upper lip and crossed her arms.

"I thought you might want to help get Naomi inside," he said. "Are you planning to have her stay downstairs, make a little bed or make up the couch? Since it's still painful for her to walk, that would be much better."

With her head cocked to the side, Lenore pursed her lips. "I don't know anything about that. The couch was made up for a bed when I got here. I assumed everything would be ready for her when she got here. I guess either that *girl* my daughter is always around, or your wife did it."

Somewhat stunned by her reply, Norwood grinned broadly and shuffled his feet. "Well, ma'am, you just give me a minute and I'll take care of things for your little girl. Now, don't you lift a finger, Okay? But if you don't mind, I'd appreciate any help you can give me with the few items she had at the hospital."

Avoiding his gaze, Lenore stepped quickly past the man, and upon seeing Naomi, she shook her head. "Tsk, tsk, poor little helpless. What were you doing all the way in Cherry Point? Does Roy know about this?"

"I'm sure he will now," Naomi muttered softly.

"Well ma'am," Norwood interrupted, "none of this is her fault, you--"

"*You* need to mind your own business, Mr. Bolton. I know you and I know your family."

"You don't know me ma'am. Now, I know your husband Al, he's a fine hardworking man, he's--"

"He's a fisherman! That's all he is. Now get my daughter out of your jalopy and--"

"Hi!" Mary Bolton called as she walked briskly from the small paved road. "I came by earlier and made the couch up downstairs, Norwood, so it's okay, but I forgot the shrimp." She giggled, "I just knew there was something I forgot, and it was the shrimp. I know how much that little gal loves shrimp." She giggled again, then walked to the front porch, pausing to touch Lenore's shoulder along the way. "It's so sweet of you to take the time to take care of your daughter-in-law. I know with you being so busy and going back and forth from Raleigh to here, well, it's got to be a lot. Thank God you're here."

Looking toward the car, she called out, "Hi Naomi, you sure do look tired, I know they don't give you much time to sleep in the hospital with all that testing and checking in on you they do." She held up a casserole dish, "I brought shrimp, you'll love it." She added more loudly, "I know your momma-in-law ain't much of a cook, so I thought I'd make you something good."

Biting the insides of her cheeks, Naomi stifled a laugh and thought, *Damn she's got nerve.*

Norwood reached into the car and grasped Naomi's arms to help her up. "Now, the doctor said you have to walk, so you walk, even if it's slow."

Naomi rose from the car seat and stood, then slowly placed one foot in front of the other.

"Who put the flowers on the dining room table?" Lenore asked as they entered. "I noticed them when I first came. Who arranged them?" Her eyes found Mary. "You? You arranged the flowers? Who taught you how to arrange flowers?"

Mary stood, hands on hips, her brow furrowed. "Lady," she began, "the cat did. Yes ma'am, the magic cat. He arranged the flowers." Her voice lilted to a popular tune. "Do you believe in magic? Dum de dum, dum dum …."

Naomi laughed aloud, then winced as she moved closer to the couch. "Thank you, Norwood, it's awfully kind of you and Mary to help me."

"We are just a phone call away," he said, inching the black phone on the end table closer. "And as for food, we'll--"

"I'll cook, no need for that," Lenore barked. "Your food is going to make her fat and she's put on enough weight as it is." Turning sharply to Naomi, she added, "My son isn't even going to recognize you if you look like a cow when he gets back."

Naomi pulled her legs up on the couch, while Mary settled a pillow beneath her head. Mary then picked up the remote control. "Must be nice, I guess it comes in real handy with you not being able to get up and change the channel."

"My son bought that for her. She sure *is* lucky to have a husband like him." Her eyes sliding to the Boltons, Lenore lifted her chin and looked toward the front door.

"Guess we'll be going now," Norward said as he tapped the wisteria pendant he had moved to the table. "For good luck and fast healing," he whispered.

Naomi's eyes met his. She knew he had been into her home without permission. Both he and Mary had, but she didn't mind. In fact, she was grateful for all they had done. Even if they were a little strange and a little nosy. They were kind and they cared. Neither kindness nor caring were things she had ever felt from her mother-in-law.

More than likely the Boltons knew about her escapade with drugs, about Elmo, and probably about the pregnancy. Even so, she supposed they would have been less judgmental than her family ever would have been. She knew they would keep her secrets. She also knew that at some point in time they would have a little chat with her.

She heard Lenore's strident voice from the kitchen and rolled her eyes.

"Poor kid, you call us if you need, okay?" Norwood winked.

Naomi grinned sarcastically. "Two weeks, that's how long the doctor said it would take before I'm up to doing things on my own." She rolled her eyes, "but I'll be damned if I don't cut that in half. I'll have that old bat out of here in a week, if not less."

****

"Hello Dillon," Lenore whispered into the phone. She smiled and laughed, returning the *I love you* she'd heard from the other end. "The little snot is lying on the couch downstairs, so I've got the bedroom." Pulling open the drawers to the dresser and bedside tables as she strolled around the room, Lenore stretched her fingers to reach far inside. She fumbled with items, pushed them aside, scoffing as she found the package of birth control pills.

"You'll never guess what I just found," she cooed to her lover, then laughed again to his response. "No, my dear, the little twit is taking birth control pills. No wonder she and Roy haven't had any babies. I wonder if he knows that she took them." She giggled and added, "He will now."

Lenore laughed again. "Yes, Dillon, I have my bathing suit … we can get the boat anytime. I don't think Little Miss Priss is going to have much to say about what I do and don't do."

Lenore plopped down on the bed, reached for the remote and just as she was crossing her legs to relax, heard her daughter-in-law call out her name.

"Oh shit, she just called out for something. Sorry darling, I better see what the spoiled brat wants. I love you so much, can't wait to see you."

Slowly descending the stairs, she asked, "What is it now?"

"I have to go to the bathroom Lenore. I need you to help me, please."

"Good Lord, Naomi," Lenore hollered as she sauntered down the stairs, "there's a bathroom five steps from you. Get up, don't be so lazy."

During the following six days, Lenore took the boat out just as many times, leaving by 9 a.m. and returning around 6 p.m. She asked to have Mary stay with Naomi during those times with instructions to make meals, do laundry and clean.

"She takes the ICW every morning, goes south. I watch her, Norwood watches her, and Juanita, at the marina says she stops there and picks up a bag of ice for the cooler every day. I bet she's meeting someone." Mary brought the cup of coffee to her lips. "She's a sneaky one, I wouldn't trust her as far as I could throw her."

"They are separated, Mary."

"But she's not supposed to be doing any hanky-panky, if you know what I mean, until she's fully divorced. And I'll bet you she's been sneaking around on her husband before they separated." Mary raised the cup to her lips again. "Is she on the phone a lot?"

"I hardly see her at all. She comes home, heats up the meal you left me and goes upstairs. I hear her laughing sometimes, so I assume she's talking to someone, and if it rings, she picks it up immediately."

"She doesn't help you do anything, not even--"

"Oh, she bought me a cane."

"A cane? Well, I guess you do need one."

"I can get myself to the bathroom okay. I'll be darned if I'm going to let her help me do that. The fuss she made the first night I was here, you wouldn't believe. She made fun of me, of my weight and accused me of so many things."

Mary raised a brow and began, "Honey, nobody is perfect, and I think you look like you've even lost some."

"You're fattening me up," Naomi giggled. "You're such a great cook."

Mary paused and searched Naomi's face. "You're a good girl, just lonely … and everybody eats too much when they're lonely. We do a lot of things when we're lonely." She sighed. "I've known miss hoity-toity since she married Roy's daddy and she's always been mean as a snake. But two can play her game. You just keep stroking that pendant and … use your head for something besides a hat rack. Catch her at her own game."

On the seventh day, a few minutes before Mary was to come, the phone rang. Naomi picked up the receiver on the first ring, just as Mary had instructed. She heard a man's voice. She heard about the trip to Atlantic Beach and the romp in the small hotel there. She heard about the trip to Beaufort the day before and plans for a trip for that day, to Emerald Isle. She heard the *I love you's* and she heard the sexual innuendo exchanged between the two. She heard, "Dillon, I'm going to take him for every cent he has."

Gag a maggot! Naomi grinned and loaded the ammunition chamber for the cat fight she knew was coming. When it would be, she wasn't sure, but she knew there would be confrontation, accusations and Naomi was not about to let Lenore get away without getting in a few rounds herself. Already, her mother-in-law had questioned her about the birth control pills, and had grilled her on going to Cherry Point. *Heaven knows what she would have said or done if she had found the pot and pills.*

"Thank God for Mim," she whispered as she slid the receiver back onto the cradle.

Feigning sleep as Lenore stepped across the floor to the back porch, Naomi waited for Mary to let herself in through the front door. It would only be moments, now, since Mary tried to schedule her comings and goings to avoid Lenore.

"I'll put the coffee on," Mary called as she entered the house. "You'd think that biddy would at least do that for you."

Naomi heard the cups rattle and other sounds of Mary as she puttered about the kitchen and thinking she was alone, opened her eyes to meet Lenore's scowling gaze.

Lenore pushed the red, floppy-brimmed hat back on her head and tugged at the starched collar of the red-striped romper she wore. Naomi's eyes rested on her mother-in-law as she stood, hands on hips, scowling at her from the back porch.

"Has the wicked witch of the East left yet?" Mary called out.

"No," Lenore called back, "I haven't left yet and I don't drink coffee, you fat cow. But I'm leaving now... have fun today," she added sarcastically. "And oh, you need to mop the floor and wash the rug. Your Majesty spilled her soup last night. It went everywhere. Did the best I could, but I know I could never clean it as good as you!"

Mary heard the back door shut and walked into the living room. "As soon as she is out of sight, you need to rub that pendant. It's right there on the table." Settling herself in the oversized chair she nodded to the pendant.

Naomi pursed her lips and scowled. "Her magic too strong for our magic, she have much bad juju. Much too powerful for simple Sloop Point woman. Ugga ugga."

"You're funny, Naomi."

Mary, you don't believe this pendant has super magic powers, do you?"

"I don't think it's going to take off and fly or turn into a toad, but I do think it offers hope. Don't you *hope* that it's magic? Hope is a powerful thing."

Naomi paused for a moment, her lips curling slyly. "It makes sense when you put it that way. Mm, magic good, ugga ugga." She tilted her head back and laughed, then rested her elbow on the arm rest of the couch. "It's going to be really funny when she finds out what I know. She thinks she has me by the hairs of my chinny chin chin, but I have a surprise for her."

Mary leaned in to listen, then stood up. "Oh, let me get the coffee and your breakfast first, I want to hear this, it's gotta be good."

Returning with a tray of coffee, cinnamon toast and fruit salad, Mary settled herself once again in the chair next to the couch. "So, what is up? What do you know?"

Naomi took a long sip from the coffee cup and bit into the cinnamon toast. She licked her lips and said,

"I heard her on the phone this morning, talking with some man named Dillon. She says she's going to take Jerry Simpson for every cent he has."

"That's going to be hard to do, if Mr. Simpson finds out about Lenore's boyfriend. I always suspected something like this was going on." Mary giggled.

"Nothing escapes you, does it Mary?"

"I just keep my eyes and ears open, honey. There's not much that gets past me."

Naomi's eyes questioned Mary's. "You know about me, don't you? You know about what--"

"I know lots of things and you need to be more careful. That's all I'll say about that right now. But we can talk about *those* things some other day.

"I'm so stupid. I'll have to tell Roy."

"Before you do that, wait. Okay?"

"Okay, I'll wait. Thank you, Mary. You and Norwood are so nice."

Mary nodded. "That family, your husband's family, has been going at it for years. Lenore ran out on him, he ran out on her. Back and forth it went for the longest time. Everybody knew about it and then things kind of settled down, or at least it got quieter, until Roy started going out with you. *She* wouldn't have it. She knew he put you before her and she wanted him to go away to college and forget all about you. Then she blamed you for him being drafted because he wasn't in college."

"That much is true. If he had gone to college--"

"You don't know what would have happened, child. My crystal ball got broken a long time ago and I know you never had one."

Naomi giggled. "I guess you're right. Besides, I know Roy has always loved working on his daddy's boats."

"And his daddy always loved having him there. I'll tell you, that man is heartbroken that his boy is overseas. Now, he thinks highly of you. I know that."

"I hardly ever see him, Mary."

"He stays busy, fishing. And he's probably got some gal in South Carolina or somewhere. He goes to Georgetown, South Carolina a lot."

"He cheats on her, she cheats on him."

"What's good for the goose is good for the gander."

"So, she'll never take his every cent, then? Not if she and Dillon are brought to light."

Holding her coffee cup close to her chest, Mary leaned back in the overstuffed chair. "Let me call Norwood. I bet he can catch her in his boat if he gets going now. He can follow her and he always carries his camera."

CHAPTER 23

"We're going scooterpootin', Ma." Mim kissed Edna on the cheek and grabbed her purse before flying out the front door. "See you this afternoon."

Edna Myers lifted the plastic clothes hamper filled with wet linens and called back, "Y'all be careful." She looked past the clothes line to the sand dunes and morning sky and thought of her daughter and how youth and life belonged to her. She laughed, recalling her own youth, when she and her husband Rufus would take the skiff to the island for a picnic, and felt the ambiguous feelings of love and loss hold her in time. She still missed him.

"I'll always miss you, Ruf," she whispered, as she took the few steps to the clothes line.

John Francis had dropped in on her a few times. *Just checking in to see if you need anything,* he had said. Robert Barns had called once to see if she might like to drive to Wilmington to see a movie. His wife had passed away eight months ago. Edna had declined.

Too soon, she'd told herself. *But just how long is long enough?* How many months or years would it take to quit missing her late husband? Then it occurred to her that it was not about whether or not she missed Rufus, it was about enjoying the life she had now. How long could she go without, when she felt the pull of laughter and friendship and closeness?

At times it felt not a month had passed since his death, but more often than not it seemed as if time had marched on, that time was way on down the road and it was leaving her behind.

Just now Mim had flown out the door to go *scooterpootin'* with friends. All of Edna's friends had husbands or they were older and settled into the rocking chair for good.

She flapped a pillowcase in the breeze and pinned it to the clothesline, then another and she watched a car of teenagers pass by on the road, laughing aloud. She watched little children trudging up the huge sand dunes less than two hundred feet from her home and saw herself as both. Remembering her days of carefree life, Edna diligently pinned the remaining linens on the line then walked into her bedroom. Pulling the bottom drawer of her dresser open, she rummaged through the items there and withdrew the only bathing suit she owned. She'd not worn it in eight years or more. She laid it on the bed.

"Oh my, that thing is as ugly as all get out." She studied the solid black tank suit and tittered, "Fiddlefart, isn't that the word I keep hearing?" Slipping out of her broad black shoes, she slipped on a lighter pair of sandals. "I'm not fiddlefarting around with any clunky old shoes anymore."

Picking up her purse, Edna shut the door behind her and walked the three blocks to the Superette and the little clothing store there.

"Lillian, fix me up. I need a new bathing suit and I don't want a black one."

Petite Lillian rounded the corner counter and padded to the bathing suit display.

"Here you go, this is all we have left this late in the season." Lillian eyed Edna for a second and asked, "Size twelve or fourteen?"

"Fourteen," Edna sighed. "I've gotten so fat."

"You're not fat, just a little plump and I think you look great for your age. You have a figure and aren't like these skinny things that walk in here." She giggled and pulled out a hanger holding a bikini. "Here you are, itsy bitsy teeny weeny."

Edna laughed, "I need more than that. How about that one piece I saw just past--"

"The one with the skirt?" Lillian asked.

"Yes, the one with the tiny little flowers."

"Just the one I was thinking of." She pulled it from the rack and handed it to Edna. "Changing room one, and call for me, I want to see you in it."

Edna nodded. "I want an honest opinion, Lil, this isn't just about a sale, you're my friend too."

****

It did look nice on her; Lillian had said so, and Edna trusted her. At home trying the suit on again, she sighed and checked the backside image of herself in the full-length mirror. The skirt covered her fanny and the tops of her thighs. Pleased and proud that she looked presentable, Edna felt the suit covered the bad parts and accentuated the better ones. Mim shared her full figure. *All the right places*, Rufus had said, and at fifty, nothing had changed much. "Just a little lower," she tittered. "A few more lumps and bumps."

She selected the yellow quilt she'd made several years back and tucked it into one of Mim's beach bags and threw a towel over her arm. She checked herself in the mirror again and borrowed a pair of Mim's flip flops. Then she too was out the door to do her own brand of scooterpootin'.

Diane and Dee Dee would meet her on the beach. Both were a few years younger than her; one was married the other newly divorced. But it was time for new friends and a different life.

CHAPTER 24

Norwood spread the pictures out across the kitchen table, smiling, chuckling unintelligible words as he did so. "And this one, you can see, and you can see it plain as day, they're smooching. He's got his hand on her derriere, excuse my French."

Naomi bent to examine the photos. Starting at the top, they exhibited a sort of slide show of the day Lenore and Dillon had spent on the boat and of their trip to Emerald Isle. Her lips spreading widely across her face, tiny bits of laughter slipped through them.

"She simply has no shame," Naomi giggled. "None at all, I swear the woman doesn't think anybody is watching the two of them."

"Glad Mary called when she did. I was heading out the door when she did and I caught Lenore just as she was going past our dock. You know, she didn't pay no mind to all to the markers, or maybe she doesn't know what's port or what's starboard,

226

but she went right through. Damn lucky she didn't run aground on something. She picked him up at Lewis Boat Yard and I hung out behind one of the little islands till he got on board and they took off. He was driving then and he stayed within the markers. Dillon? Is that his name?"

Both Mary and Naomi nodded.

"And they went to Emerald Isle?" Naomi asked.

Norwood nodded. "Yep, I got out, followed them a bit as they strolled around, then ate some lunch, kissin' and holding hands the whole time. I got plenty of pictures of that." He chuckled and added, "After the last picture, I went on back to my boat, drove up to Jacksonville and put my film in at Walgreens."

"What was their last picture?" Naomi asked.

Norwood reached into his shirt pocket and laid the photo in front of her. Naomi picked it up.

"It's the two of them checking in to the Tides Motel."

"Are you going to listen to any more of her phone calls?" Mary asked.

Naomi shook her head no. "I just don't think I want to listen to Lenore and her boyfriend again. What's the point? It's gratifying already to know that I got her."

"By the hair of her chinny chin, chin," Mary tittered.

"But I feel badly for Roy, he's had to put up with his parents all these years and now I think of how this is going to do a number on him."

"Don't worry about him," Norwood started. "When he gets back, he'll be working with his father. He knows how things are and you have ammunition against Lenore now, she won't be taking Jerry to the cleaners."

"She doesn't even realize or even care that if she takes her husband to the cleaners how it will affect his fishing business and even her own son."

"Bag of worms," Norwood commented. "That's what she is." He looked to Naomi, "Where's your pendant?"

"She keeps it on the end table next to the couch," Mary cooed.

Norwood rushed from the kitchen, returning moments later with the pendant in his hand, whispering words Naomi could not decipher.

"He's always loved that boy," Mary said.

Naomi shook her head and exhaled a long sigh, "Sometimes y'all ...."

"It's spreading the wishing, spreading the hope," Mary explained, her face deadpan. "What's it hurt Naomi? Who are we hurting with the way we do things? And contrary to some folks' saying, we don't do no drugs."

Reaching her hand to pat Mary's shoulder, Naomi answered, "You don't hurt anybody, not a single soul. You're allowed to be as weird as you want, Mary. All I know is you've done nothing but try to help me and my husband."

Mary nodded and mouthed a thank you. "Best thing you can do is show these pictures to that old bat. They're going to be the best juju on her."

Naomi nodded a yes.

"Now, I'd love to be a fly on the wall when you do, that would be a hoot."

"You can be a fly in the kitchen."

Pulling a chair out from the table, Norwood sat and asked, "When do you expect her home?"

Naomi shrugged. "Beats me. She usually shows up sometime between six and seven but then she'll come slinking in around eight or nine sometimes, too."

"Don't mention a thing," Norwood rubbed the pendant briskly, "but tomorrow morning I want you to try and listen in on her. Mary, you come in early and I'm going to be standing out by the dock and the boat. I'll make sure she ain't got no gas in the thing." Norwood slid his fingers across the pendant more slowly. "I watched her gas up at Lewis's marina yesterday afternoon, she does that every afternoon when she takes lover boy back."

****

Naomi waited for the phone to ring the next morning, but to her surprise it did not. Instead, Lenore pranced down the stairs, still in her night shirt and with her hair in rollers. She called a cheery good morning to Naomi and walked into the kitchen, where she found Mary already having prepared the coffee and now working on a breakfast of fried potatoes, onions and eggs.

Sprinkling bits of grated cheese into the mixture, Mary slid her eyes to the woman as she settled herself at the kitchen table. "Not going out this morning for your daily boat ride?"

"Oh, I thought I'd hang around the house with you two lovelies and enjoy your cooking. By the looks of you, it must be absolutely delicious. "Sliding a finger onto the rim of the cup of coffee Mary handed her, Lenore lit a cigarette.

"We don't smoke in this house, it stinks. Makes people who do it stink, of course in your case it might make you smell better."

A deep, throaty laugh escaped Lenore and she pulled heavily on the cigarette again. "I hope you have an ashtray."

Mary slid a saucer to her. "I hear it's bad for you, might lead you to an early grave."

"Oh, I'll just get myself one of those purple pendants like you gave Naomi and conjure myself out of any ill health problems. Isn't that what you two nuts do? Ooh, ghosts and goblins and magic spells," Lenore mocked. "It's all evil what you do. Everybody knows how crazy y'all are. Just because you own a little bit of land around here you might think that you and Norwood are important and maybe even liked a little in this community. But I tell you one thing, people laugh at you. They laugh at you all the time!"

"Oh, like you're not made fun of, you … you … whore!"

"Who are you calling a whore?" Lenore rose from the table. "I ought to--"

"Hey! What's all the yelling about in there?" Naomi limped into the kitchen, her cane in hand.

"This fat cow has to go. I don't care how much she helps you and it looks to me that you are doing pretty good anyway. Look, you can get around just fine. In fact, I don't think you need me around here anymore either."

"You don't do anything for her, you're gone all day," Mary spouted.

Naomi leaned against the table and settled into a chair. "Now Mary, I think her being gone has given me the opportunity to be more self-reliant. I'm grateful that she has been so useless."

"I'm getting out of here, packing my stuff and I'm gone. I don't need you two telling me--well, why after all I've done to help you out, I came all the way from Raleigh to help my *poor defenseless daughter-in-law*. What were you doing in Cherry Point anyway? Have you been cheating on my son while he's away fighting in a war you sent him to? I'm telling him--telling him everything!"

Naomi reached into her robe pocket and pulled out the packet of pictures. She laid them on the table and quickly dealt them in order. "Here's you and Dillon at Lewis Boatyard, here's you and Dillon on the ICW, here's you and Dillon with his hand on your ass, here's you and Dillon kissing, here you are eating lunch at a restaurant in Emerald Isle, here are you and lover boy, checking into the Tides Motel. Here, here you are, bitch. Think you're going to take your husband for everything he has? Think again, you self-centered witch. You're more evil than either of the Boltons! Planning to destroy your husband, doing your witchy wiles with Dillon. So don't give me your bullshit about Mary and Norwood, they've been kinder and more helpful to me than you've ever been."

Lenore bent to scoop up the pictures, quickly gathering them in her hands.

"Take them, take them all, use them as mementos," Mary said. "I have copies, lots of copies and negatives, you old crow. And by the way, you look like a bag of bones in your bikini. Your spine sticks out of your back and your legs look like toothpicks." Mary called as Lenore walked from the kitchen. "And oh yeah, you need to pluck those hairs on your chinny, chin, chin."

Naomi and Mary sat quietly, sipping coffee and listening to Lenore bang things around upstairs. Muffled cursing drifted downstairs and the two women giggled as they waited for the *long*-awaited departure of Lenore Simpson.

Finally, it came. Not daring to make her exit through the front door, Lenore slammed the backdoor behind her, hollering as she walked, more obscenities that could not be heard well enough to decipher.

"I guess she's got a bee in her bonnet," Mary giggled.

"That's one hissy fit she's having," Naomi tittered.

"Wonder what she's going to do with the pictures?" Mary asked.

"You do have copies?"

"Yes siree, I have copies and I have the negatives and as soon as Mr. Simpson gets back up here from South Carolina, I'm showing them to him. And I think you ought to tell him about that phone call you heard."

"I don't know him all that well, not well enough for that."

"This isn't about friendship, Naomi, this is business. If he didn't have all the information he needs, that old bag of worms could really try to take all he has. I'm sure she has some sort of proof that Jerry runs out on her. I've even heard a rumor that your husband has a half-brother down there in Georgetown."

Lifting her head to question Mary, Naomi asked, "Really? A half-brother?"

"Or sister, I don't know for sure. All I know is it's what's been going around for the last fifteen years."

"That's bad."

"If she hadn't had a hysterectomy, she'd done have given birth twenty times over, believe me. I'm telling Lenore she's a whore ...." Mary giggled. "Rhymes, doesn't it?"

CHAPTER 25

Roy hadn't decided whether or not to call and let Naomi know he was on his way home. He hadn't decided if he wanted to surprise her or not. He wasn't too sure of anything these days, especially since that day he'd been misinformed about a bombing target.

Women and children. He couldn't get it out of his head. *No, it's clear.* He'd been given the order and the target and then he'd asked again about the certainty of the target being viet cong. *It's clear, no noncoms, it's charley.*

He leaned over and kissed Duyen softly on the lips. He wasn't sure about this either. In all the time he'd been in Nam he'd never cheated on Naomi. He'd never even considered it. After all the cheating he'd seen his parents do over the years, all the arguments and screaming, he'd sworn he'd never do it, he'd never cheat on his wife. He loved her more than anything. She had been his rock over the last two years.

Rolling to his back, he folded his arms behind his head and gazed at the ceiling of the small room where he lay. Had he written last or had Naomi? It seemed their letters had become more infrequent, but then, there had been little to say. So much had been on his mind.

He reached to the side table and pulled the bottle of warm beer towards his lips. He rested it there. The liquid poured slowly down his throat and Roy closed his eyes again. *So why am I here lying in bed with this chink, this Vietnamese gal who I pay? I pay so she can support herself and her kid.*

His fingers touching her thick straight hair, he pulled a strand from the side of her face. *She is pretty*, he thought. *And maybe I could love her.*

Duyen turned to him, her small fingers stroking the sides of his stubbled face. Her eyes met his and held for a moment before the sound of her young child echoed from the corner of the room. She rose, not bothering to cover herself, and walked to gather her baby from the dresser drawer she'd made into a bed.

Wonder who the father is? Roy asked himself. *It could be anybody.* It was funny how he felt no ill feeling for this young girl and her illegitimate baby. He didn't judge, couldn't do that to anyone, not after what he had done. Reaching once again for the bottle, he pressed it to his lips and let it rest against his chest, sipping now and then.

With the baby now laying between them, Roy stroked Duyen's hair and kissed her forehead, took another swig from the bottle and sighed. It seemed to fill the room, this sigh, signifying the beginning and ending of everything he'd known in the last year.

As he rose and dressed, he dug into the pocket of his pants and pulled out a handful of MPCs and laid them on the side table. It wasn't much, but they might transfer into fifty or so dollars, enough for the woman to feed her child for a while.

"I know you don't understand anything I say," he began, "but I want to thank you for being here for me. I hope this money will help you and your child. I have to go now. I am going back to my home in the states."

****

Naomi was kneeling near the flower garden in the front yard, weeding the periwinkles and petunias. Her thoughts had folded back to the short few months when she had been taking drugs, and she wondered why she had ever done so.

Mary had told her that the reason for her *misstep* was because she hadn't been ready to face reality, and that running away from the news and avoiding the subject of Roy being in Vietnam was not the best way to deal with the situation. Mary had spoken to her like the mother Naomi wished she'd always had, one who was confident and would stand up to adversity.

Shaking her head, thinking of the last time she and her mother had spoken, Naomi bit her lip. It had been right after the accident; her father had never bothered to call or even acknowledge anything. Since then, Adele had called twice and met her in Jacksonville at Sears once. But the communication had been slight and only apologetic on her mother's part as she explained how much she wished things were different.

Well, why don't you make it different, Mom? Naomi had begun, but the look on her mother's face had stopped the reprimand short. She knew things would never change.

Naomi talked with Mary about that, too.

"She has to want to change things. And maybe you are not so different than your mother, Naomi. You shut out the war, the whole war. Sometimes we hide the ugly things so we don't have to deal with them."

"I still don't like the war," Naomi retorted.

"How about Roy? Do you still like him? He's been fighting in that war."

"I love Roy."

"Well … how are you going to deal with that?"

The thought of the conversations with Mary brought a smile to Naomi's face. Mary was a ray of sunshine, a voice of reason and there she was, odd as a duck out of water. Yes, some folks ridiculed Mary and Norwood, but it was they who had come to her rescue. It was they who accepted her the way she was.

"I will accept my husband, I will love him and provide support for his choices," she whispered as she moved the trowel among the weeds.

Standing, removing the gardening gloves from her hands, Naomi rested her hands on her hips and bent backward. She felt the muscles of her back pull and relax. Her face turned toward the sun, she giggled and thought of Lenore and the photos and Jerry Cartwright. That whole scene had changed. "Oh, what a tangled web we weave," she began, and then she felt hands gently covering her eyes.

"Guess who," came the familiar voice of her husband.

He twirled her to face him and, holding her face in his hands, Roy kissed her cheeks, her forehead and her lips. "Oh, baby, I've missed you so much."

"Oh my gosh, I'm so glad to see you! I've missed you so much, so much you have no idea." Naomi kissed him long and held onto him as he nuzzled her neck and face. "Why didn't you tell me you were coming home on leave? I wondered why I hadn't heard from you in so long."

Roy paused for a split second and let his fingers stroke her thick, long hair. "I'm not on leave. I'm out. Out for good. We can start over again. We can start everything over again."

"Is the war over?"

"For me it is."

CHAPTER 26

Mim had heard the news: Roy was home, all was right with Naomi's world, and Mim was glad. It had been one hell of a year with going to Miller Motte. Thank goodness graduation was next week. She wondered what kind of job she would look for and she thought about Naomi. *Probably won't be looking for anything real soon.* Mim giggled at the thought of the couple. "I hope they're happy. I hope she never tells him about what happened ... or should she?" Mim cocked her head to the side and weighed Naomi's options. "How do you know what to do?" she asked aloud.

Her eyes slid to her mother, peacefully rocking in her chair as she watched *Bonanza* on television. Edna had finally gotten a color television, and one with a remote control, too. That wasn't the only thing her mother had purchased as of late. It appeared she had purchased a whole new wardrobe. Gone were the dark, heavy shoes she'd always worn, and in their place were sandals and some colorful pumps. Her hairdo was different as well. Having cut it a few inches shorter, Edna now wore her hair in a bob with bangs.

She'd become more active, not only at church affairs but with friends. She went to the movies in Wilmington, went bowling there too, and had even gone to the beach with a couple of her friends a few times.

Things were changing and it all looked like it was for the good. Except for the times she listened to the nightly news and heard about the ongoing and escalating war in Vietnam. Except for those times, life seemed good to Mim.

Roger still came by about once a week, and they walked on the beach or sat and talked at the blue house, but there had been no movement toward romance. For now, Mim was cool with that. She knew he was still visiting ladies in Jacksonville, or at least she suspected it. Either way, it did not matter. She had lost her interest in falling in love with Roger, for the present, and was now enjoying their friendship.

It was obvious that he had mixed feelings about Vietnam. He expressed guilt about leaving his buddies behind and doubt that his job with the Jacksonville Police Department was one he wanted to pursue further.

"If I'd only gotten to know Anthony as well as I know you," she said to him, one evening. "I don't think I would have married him. I really didn't know him at all."

"It takes a long time to get to know someone," Roger said, while he leaned against the side of the house. "I still don't know what I want and I still don't understand all that I've seen and been through."

She wanted to touch his cheek, caress him. Not like a lover, but like a child. Sometimes he seemed so lost.

Instead, she reached for his hand and gently squeezed Roger's fingers. "I want you to be happy."

"That would be nice." His eyes finding hers, Roger leaned in to kiss Mim's forehead. "You know, we could have ended up enemies if I would have let you have your way."

Mim nodded. "Yeah, I was on the rebound."

"I'm happy that you and I are friends now."

"Good friends."

He paused for a moment, looked out over the blue ocean and returned the squeeze of her hand. "I like it here. I like this blue house."

"I always wanted to live here when I was a kid," Mim said wistfully.

"It was right here at this house, the first time we spoke to each other."

Mim nodded. "Yeah, I thought you were some kind of weirdo, sneaking around here."

Laughing, Roger rose and ran his fingers along the banister of the porch. Holding her gaze, he blurted, "I've reenlisted. I leave tomorrow. I just wanted to tell you how much your friendship has meant to me."

There was no sense in denying the pain, the overwhelming feeling that something dear and part of her was disappearing. Despite all they've been through, Mim considered Roger a calming force. He made her think about things and not simply react.

Mim's eyes filled with tears and she stood next to him, leaning against his body. "Damn I'll miss you."

"I'll miss you. I'll write."

"No, you won't."

He shrugged.

"You have it good, here on this little island."

"You could stay." Her eyes begged.

"I'm no good for anybody now. I've got to do this."

Mim nodded, wrapped her arms around his neck and held herself close to him.

Roger reciprocated and, smoothing her hair away from her face, kissed her lips.

"I love you."